Vacation at Sunshine Farm

The Third Summer

Andrea Freund

The Third Summer

Translated by Karen Nickel Anhalt

Copyright: © Andrea Freund 2010
Translated by Karen Nickel Anhalt
Original title: Freiheit auf vier Hufen
Cover and inside illustrations: © Eleonore Gerhaher
Cover layout: © Stabenfeldt AS

Typeset by Roberta L. Melzl
Editor: Bobbie Chase
Printed in Germany, 2010

ISBN: 978-1-934983-47-8

Stabenfeldt, Inc.
225 Park Avenue South
New York, NY 10003
www.pony4kids.com

Available exclusively through PONY.

Horseback riding camp in idyllic Upper Marlboro for boys and girls, 8-16 years of age. Affectionate care, exceptionally beautiful grounds for trail rides and riding instructions with well-trained ponies and horses guaranteed. Lodgings in our picturesque farmhouse. All guests will have their own horse or pony to care for. Contact: Marty Sunshyne, sunshine@horsemail.com, Tel. ...

Chapter 1

"Riding camp?"

Mrs. Hendricks looked at her daughter, utterly flabbergasted.

"But April, you know that ..." she struggled to find the words.

April felt her face go hot with anger and despair. "What? That I'm a cripple who can never ride again?" she yelled.

"April!"

Mrs. Hendricks's voice sounded shrill for a moment, but then she managed to compose herself. "Honey," she continued quietly. "You know that's not something I would ever say."

"Oh yeah?" April laughed bitterly. "What else would you call a person who can't walk any more?" She clumsily heaved herself into the wheelchair that stood

6

directly next to her bed. She sat down slowly and looked at her mother with blazing eyes. "A cripple. That's what they call someone like me. And anyway, even if people don't come out and say it, that's what they're thinking. You've told me yourself that I can never ride again."

April paused a moment and looked out the window into the garden, where Xavier, her Labrador, frolicked on the lawn. How she wished she could go run with him.

"That's ridiculous." April's mother slowly took a few steps forward and stretched out her arms. "It's just that ..." She sighed as she pushed aside the horse magazines that were spread across the bed and sat down. "Try to understand that your father and I worry about you – after all that has happened."

April closed her eyes and put her hands over her ears. She didn't want to hear what her mother had to say. She didn't want to think about her accident. Didn't want to think about the screeching tires. The horrible crash. Bonaparte's shrill whinny. A shudder ran through her entire body.

When she more or less had a grip on herself again, she lowered her arms slowly and said in a quiet, steady voice, "I know that it hasn't been easy for you and Dad either, but I can't bear not being around horses anymore. Can't you understand that? I ... I ..." Her eyes welled with tears and she began to sob loudly. Her mother went over to her, bent down and held her tightly.

"Oh sweetheart," she said, gently stroking her daughter's hair, "I'm just so sorry about everything. I wish I could help you somehow."

"Then let me ride again, Mom. Please."

"But can't we just look around nearby first, to see if someone in our area has a gentle horse? Does it really have to be riding camp? You'd be away from home for an entire week. I don't think that ..."

"That they would accept someone like me?"

"April!" Mrs. Hendricks knelt in front of April and looked deep into her eyes. "Now you listen to me. I don't want to hear you talking like that. You are a perfectly normal person, just like everyone else."

"Then why can't I go there?" April asked and wrinkled her forehead. "Why don't you just call them and ask if they'll take someone like me?"

"April!"

"Okay, okay." April raised her hand in a placating gesture. "Just please try to understand, Mom, that I can't live without horses."

"My goodness, April, when you set your heart on something …" April's mother stood up and smiled sadly. "All right then, I'll call them and ask if they have a suitable horse for you. If I could only understand why, of all things, you are so intent on going to riding camp."

April watched her mother as she left the room. She didn't quite know the answer to that question herself. She guided her wheelchair over to the bed and picked up the magazine that had the advertisement. "Affectionate care, exceptionally beautiful grounds for trail rides and riding instructions with well-trained ponies and horses guaranteed," she read in a low voice. "All guests will have their own horse or pony

to care for." It sounded exactly like what April had always dreamed of. But was that the only reason? After all, she really could take her mother's advice and look for a horse to ride nearby if she were so desperate to ride again. April shook her head. No, that wasn't the only reason. Now that she thought about it, she also liked the idea of being away from home for a week. She loved her parents and knew that they would do anything for her. Still, no matter how hard her mother and her father tried, April could sense how hard it was for them to deal with her new situation, and how sad both of them were since her horrible accident.

The accident.

April bit her lower lip. Just don't think about it again. Even if the thought of going to a riding camp and being alone for a week was a little scary, she needed to get away. Needed to go somewhere else and to leave everything behind her. April leaned back in her wheelchair and sighed deeply. Simply leave everything behind her. That would be nice. But why was she even spending so much time thinking about it? She could already guess what the people at – what was it called again? – Sunshine Farm would say. Surely there wasn't any room for someone like her.

Chapter 2

"A horse for riding therapy?"

June shook her head. "Did I hear you right – you want to use Modena for riding therapy?"

"Of course. What's wrong with that?" asked Marty. The question clearly offended her and she slammed the dishwasher closed. "Modena is very well-behaved."

"That's true." June rubbed her chin thoughtfully and followed her mother as she stormed off to the living room. "I know she's well-behaved, but is that enough? I mean, um, don't those kinds of horses have to have special training?"

"Oh, that." Marty blew a lock of her red hair out of her face and pulled a book off the bookshelf in front of her. "Everything we need to know is right in here." She waved the book, which was entitled, "Equine Assisted Activity and Therapy," under June's nose.

"Ugh."

June plunked herself down into one of their comfortable overstuffed chairs.

"You don't really believe that all you have to do to train a horse for riding therapy is to read a few pages in a book, do you? Modena is a terrific jumper and she's terrific for riding lessons too, but riding therapy? That's totally different."

"First and foremost these horses have to be calm and even-tempered, and Modena is surely all that," said Marty sharply. "Or are you saying that's not the case?"

"No, no," June said quickly. Marty tended to get pretty unpleasant if anyone criticized her beloved mare. "It's just that, well, if anything bad happened then that could become a serious problem for Sunshine Farm, don't you think? Especially now that things are going so well for us."

June was right. Ever since Mr. Schultz, the father of her friend Charly, had become a partner in Sunshine Farm, Marty suddenly had more campers than she knew what to do with.

"Hmm."

Marty sat down in the chair across from her and looked out the window, lost in thought. "Besides, you don't have any kind of training in riding therapy at all," June continued. "I think you should pass on this one."

"Do you really think so?" Marty slid around nervously in her armchair and grinned sheepishly.

The alarm bells went off in June's head.

"Wait a second, are you trying to tell me that you've already confirmed it?"

Marty nodded.

June couldn't believe it. Once again she had to ask herself why it was that she had to reprimand her mother and not the other way around. Sometimes Marty acted like an immature child, while her daughter had to be the responsible one.

"Must you always agree to something first and think it over later?" June groaned.

Marty smiled pitifully.

"The woman who called sounded so friendly that I didn't want to disappoint her. She called for her daughter, who had an accident and has been in a wheelchair ever since. Come on, June, you know what I'm like. I just couldn't say no."

June sighed. She certainly did know what her mother was like! If Marty had an idea, then she never thought it over for very long – she just went ahead and did it. Her mother was truly an excellent horsewoman and riding instructor, but she wasn't a riding therapist!

"Can't you just call them back and explain to them that it's just not possible?"

"June, please. How will that sound? You don't really want me to call and tell her that I made a mistake? No, there's no way I can do that."

Marty shook her head with determination.

"But you could tell them that your therapy horse came down with something. Please, Mom. You'll think of something."

Marty thought it over for a moment. Then a huge smile spread across her face.

"You know what? I'll bet there are plenty of trained

riding therapists in this area who would come to our farm. I can start asking around right now to find someone who could come here that week to work with the girl."

"With which horse? You still don't have a trained therapy horse."

"Calm down, will you? I have a feeling that Modena would do an excellent job. Once I've found a therapist, he or she can come to the farm right away to have a look at Modena. I'll bet my sweet horse will be able to do the job without a hitch."

"All right, then," June sighed and stood up. She knew her mother much too well to believe that she would change her mind. "I just hope you're right and that your 'sweet horse' really will be up to the task."

"She will, you'll see," Marty grinned confidently and grabbed the telephone from the living room table.

"Where do you want to go now, June?"

"I already told you that. I plan to go for a trail ride with Nelson."

"Oh my," said Marty contritely. "I'm sorry, honey, but I'm afraid that's not possible."

"And why not?"

"Because you have to muck out the stables."

"Why me? I thought you were going to do it."

"I thought so, too," Marty said and groaned as if the entire weight of the world were on her shoulders. "But I have to start making phone calls to find a riding therapist. You know how it is – business before pleasure."

Without waiting for an answer she sauntered into her

office and shut the door behind her. June stood there, looking crestfallen as she stared at the closed office door. If only her mother weren't so impulsive. But then again, if her mother weren't like that, they wouldn't be living on Sunshine Farm today. June looked out of the window and saw Nelson, her beloved Anglo-Arabian, grazing peacefully on the paddock. As far as June was concerned there was no nicer place in the world than the farm outside of Washington, DC, that she and her mother had moved to after her parents' divorce.

All right then, she'd muck out instead of going on a trail ride. On second thought, June wasn't all that upset. As long as she could be around horses, she was happy to do just about anything. She whistled a happy tune as she walked down the stairs to the entrance hall and pulled on her stable shoes. Then she opened the door to the courtyard and breathed in the mild spring air. It was unusually warm for late March. The sky was a brilliant blue, the birds were chirping and she could see their horses frolicking in the paddocks.

"Hi, June!"

Marty's friend Bea was leading Princess, her graceful Trakehner mare, to the hitching post. She gave June a friendly wave. "I think Princess rolled around in every mud puddle that she could find today."

June laughed. It looked like every inch of the lovely mare's entire body was covered in dirt.

"Where's your mother? I was thinking that maybe we could go for a little trail ride together."

"I'm afraid not," said June regretfully. "Mom is in a rush to find a riding therapist."

"A riding therapist?"

Bea raised her eyebrows and looked skeptical.

"What is Marty up to this time?"

June told her about the phone call and that Marty didn't have the heart to disappoint the woman.

"Well, that's typical of your mother," groaned Bea. "She doesn't know how to say no. But I'm glad you were able to talk her out of giving the lessons herself. I don't even want to think about what could happen if something went wrong. Would your insurance policy even cover it?"

Bea was a tax accountant and she was always thinking about the importance of ensuring that everything went according to plan. In other words, she was the exact opposite of Marty, who didn't think things over until after the fact.

"I have no idea." June shrugged her shoulders. "One thing's for sure though, there's no way that we'll be able to change her mind about going ahead with it. You know what Mom is like when she makes up her mind about something ..."

"... Then she'll follow through with it," Bea completed the sentence with a laugh as she fished the currycomb out of her cleaning kit. "All right, then it looks like I'll be riding alone, assuming I'll be able to get this animal of mine clean first." She scrutinized Princess, whose coat gave off a cloud of dust every time she moved. "If you ask me, she looks more like a wild boar than a horse, don't you think?"

June was about to answer her when she noticed a car coming up their driveway. The car stopped in front of the stable and a boy got out. She had completely forgotten that she and her friend Ben had planned to go on a trail ride together!

"Hi June!" Ben slammed the car door behind him and walked over to her. "This sure is perfect weather for a trail ride, don't you think?"

"I'm sorry, Ben, but it's not going to happen for me," said June apologetically. "Mom just got another of her brilliant ideas, which is why I get to muck out the stable." Ben had such a quizzical expression on his face that June quickly told him everything.

"If that's the way it is, then I'll give you a hand. If we hurry, maybe we'll still have time for a short ride."

June gratefully accepted his offer and sure enough, with Ben's help, the stable and paddocks were mucked out so quickly that they really did have time for a trail ride. Björn, the Icelandic gelding that Ben cared for, was in the process of shedding his winter coat and the hair blew across the entire farm by the light breeze.

"I could practically knit a sweater with all that," said Ben after he had swept most of it up. "Just think, that way I could have Björn with me all the time." He tenderly scratched the gelding behind his ears. "You see, these robust Icelandics have their own unique advantages."

June laughed. She was fond of the Icelandic, and while she didn't have anything against the robust breeds, her heart belonged to the sensitive warmbloods like her

Anglo-Arabian gelding, Nelson. She gently ran her hand over her white horse's silky coat. "Nothing against your Icelandic, but I wouldn't trade my Nelson for any other horse in the world."

"And I would never have expected you to," said Ben as he tightened Björn's girth. "Now why don't you swing up on your dream horse so that we can finally get going? And try to restrain yourself a little, okay? Otherwise my sturdy Björn will get mad at your noble steed."

June promised to keep her Nelson under control on the stretch where they galloped. She knew well enough that the Icelandic couldn't stand being left behind when they galloped and he would start to buck to express his displeasure. In fact, Ben had been unseated in a less than gentle manner twice recently.

As they were beginning to set off they encountered Bea, who was just returning from her own trail ride with Princess.

"Is your mother still upstairs?" she asked.

June nodded.

"Then I'll go straight up to her so that I can talk over meal plans for the week after next."

"Why does Bea want to talk about camp meals with your mother?" Ben asked after they had resumed riding.

"Maxi and Lena are flying to Spain with their parents during this vacation. And you don't for a minute believe that my mom wants to cook for our camp guests herself, do you?"

Ben laughed out loud. Marty was a terrific horsewoman, but in the kitchen she was practically useless. For that reason, Cheryl Morris, the mother of June's friends, Maxi and Lena, had been doing the cooking for the campers.

"No way, I don't believe that. But I'll bet that if she did do the cooking, you'd never have any riding camp guests again! And I doubt that Charly's rich dad would be pleased if his partner started poisoning the customers."

"You see what I mean? That's why Bea jumped in to help. She even took a week's vacation so that she could be here the entire time. It'll be a huge relief for us since not only is Bea a good cook, she can also lead trail rides and give lessons. I know we'll have a lot of fun with her."

"Oh yes, the camp guests." Ben let his gaze sweep across the paddocks. "I wonder what'll happen this time."

Chapter 3

"She has *what*?"

June couldn't believe her ears.

"You heard right." Marty sank down onto a kitchen chair with a groan. "Bea has chicken pox."

"Isn't she, er, I mean, um, maybe a little too old for that?" Up until that moment, June had always thought that only children came down with the chicken pox.

"She didn't have the chicken pox when she was a kid, and she must have caught it from her niece who visited her last week. At any rate, Bea is out of commission for the next two weeks and she definitely won't be able to cook when the camp kids are here."

"Oh, no!"

"You can say that again. Now what am I supposed to do?"

Marty looked at June beseechingly.

"Say, June, do you think maybe you could...?"

June shook her head resolutely.

"No way, Mom. Anything, just not cooking. You can forget about that."

"But what will we do? I can't possibly cancel out on all the kids."

"Maybe Charly's dad can help. He knows so many people. He could hire someone to do the cooking."

"No way." Marty wrung her hands anxiously. "Just think about how much money that would cost. You know that we have to keep our costs down if the farm is going to turn a profit."

Before June could respond, the phone rang. Marty got up.

"We'll talk about this later, okay?"

Her mother left the kitchen and June went over to the window to think things over.

They needed to find a solution quickly, because the camp guests would arrive the following week. But no matter how hard she thought about it, she couldn't come up with anything. Then her cell phone rang.

"Hi, June." It was her friend Charly, the daughter of Marty's business partner.

"How are you doing, Charly?"

"Good. Especially since it won't be long before I finally get to go to your place. I miss Nano so much."

Nano was one of Sunshine Farm's five Haflingers. He was originally meant to be used for riding lessons,

but then Charly's father bought the horse for his daughter.

"I know what you mean. I can't even imagine not seeing Nelson for such a long time."

Charly lived in Washington, D.C., so she only spent time at Sunshine Farm on the weekends, but she had to stay home over the last weekend because she had a bad cold. "It's just miserable. But he has a much nicer life out there with you than he would in a stable closer to where we live. At least at Sunshine Farm he can spend all day outside and move around freely."

"And he certainly moves around a lot," June laughed. "A few days ago I barely managed to keep the Haflinger Gang from slipping through the fence to run off and mess up Farmer Myers' field."

While the farmer who lived next to Sunshine Farm was no longer at war with June and Marty, he wasn't especially pleased when the Haflingers broke out and trampled his fields.

"I can hardly wait for vacation to start ... how about you?"

"I guess, but ..." June stammered.

"But what?"

June thought for a minute. Should she tell Charly that Bea had come down with chicken pox and wouldn't be able to cook for the camp guests? Maybe Marty didn't want Mr. Schultz to find out about that. On the other hand, Charly was her best friend and they didn't keep any secrets from each other.

"Remember how Bea was planning to help out with the cooking because Cheryl Morris is away on vacation? Well, now she can't because she has chicken pox."

"Chicken pox?" Charly blurted out in surprise. "But I thought only kids got that."

"That's what I thought too, but Bea never had it when she was a kid and now she caught it from her niece."

"That's really a problem," said Charly. "So who's going to do the cooking? Not your mother, I hope!"

"No," sighed June. "No need to worry about that. But we have no idea who can help us out." She paused briefly and then continued. "Please don't tell your Dad about it, okay? I have the feeling that Mom's worried that he'll think she's unprofessional for coming to him with problems like that."

"Don't worry," said Charly. "He's got better things to do at the moment." June thought she could hear a touch of bitterness in her voice. "He flew to the Bahamas with his girlfriend and there's no way I'm going to call him there."

"Oh. I understand."

June didn't know what she should say to that. It had to be really hard on Charly, knowing that her father had a new girlfriend so soon after her parents split up.

"It's okay," said Charly darkly. "Let's just not talk about it. You know what? I'll ask my mother. Maybe she has an idea."

"That would be great," said June, although she couldn't picture Charly's mother being a big help in this case. Vanessa Schultz was a very nice lady, but in June's opinion she was far too elegant and sophisticated to spend any time thinking about a subject as mundane as cooking for a bunch of kids at riding camp. June always felt a little self-conscious around her, as if she hadn't combed her hair just right or might have a stain on her T-shirt.

"Hey, I have to go now," said Charly. "Our doorbell just rang and it's probably my piano teacher. See you."

"See you," said June and set aside her cell phone. "My piano teacher," she repeated softly. Sometimes she felt as if she knew only one Charly – the Charly who visited her at Sunshine Farm. In contrast, Charly's life in Georgetown, one of the most exclusive neighborhoods in Washington, seemed so foreign to her and even a little alarming.

"Oh June, you do have to clear the table, you know," said Marty as she walked back into the kitchen. She blew a fire-red strand of hair out of her face.

"Why me? You know that I was planning to practice some jumps on the green with Nelson."

"You can still do that later," Marty said reassuringly. "I need to hurry down to groom Modena. The riding therapist will be here any minute. Please don't be angry with me, but you know that business comes before pleasure."

She breathed a kiss in June's hair and then raced downstairs. June heard the door slam shortly after.

This riding therapy business was slowly starting

to bug her! Her mother didn't seem to have time for anything else. And the problem of who would be doing the cooking still hadn't been solved. June sighed and began clearing the dirty plates from the table. She made a lot of noise putting them into the dishwasher.

Chapter 4

"June, this is Mrs. Wendt. Mrs. Wendt, this is my daughter, June."

June eyeballed the short, stocky woman with the wild blonde curls who had just gotten out of the ancient bright yellow VW beetle that was parked next to the stable.

"Just call me Ines; then I won't feel too old." The woman gave June a firm handshake and smiled at her with sparkling eyes. June liked her immediately.

"And this here is Modena." Marty turned around and gestured toward the beautifully groomed dark brown mare that was standing next to the hitching post, dozing in the sun.

"So you're the therapy horse."

Ines approached Modena and gently stroked her coat, which glistened in the sunshine.

"You are a really beautiful animal."

She turned back to Marty and June.

"What kind of training does she have?"

"Modena performed up to Level 2 in Jumping and Level 1 in Dressage," said Marty proudly. "I trained her myself. She was a very successful tournament horse, but now I only ride her here at home. She's still in good form, though. I recently did a few jumps with her and you could tell how much fun she still had doing that."

"Aha," said Ines, sounding everything but impressed. "And what else?"

"And what else?"

Marty gaped at her.

"What do you mean, 'and what else?'"

"Tell me about her training as a therapy horse."

"Training as a therapy horse?"

Marty had no idea what she was talking about.

"I mean, what has she done so far in terms of riding therapy?"

"Oh that's what you meant. Well, um, she, er – well I suppose she hasn't really done anything yet as a therapy horse. But she's very gentle, isn't that right, June?"

Marty gave June a desperate look. June nodded vigorously.

"She really is very gentle. During camp we always use her for lessons and she does that very well."

"For lessons, I see."

Ines rubbed her chin, deep in thought, and turned back to Modena.

"Well, she certainly does give the impression of being

28

even-tempered, but I would have preferred her having some experience with riding therapy. If I understood correctly, the girl who is arriving next week is a paraplegic. Having a rider like that is a completely new experience for Modena and we don't know how she'll behave in that kind of a situation. Aside from that, she looks quite big."

"She's 16.3 hands," Marty croaked nervously.

"Well, think about it. We'll have to help the girl onto the horse and that's not easy with a horse this tall. How old did you say the girl was?"

"Twelve years old, just like June," Marty answered and pointed to her daughter.

"Hmm." Ines looked at June for a moment and then smiled. "Do you think you could do me a favor, June?"

"Yes, er, sure. What do you need?"

"Before I know if I can work with Modena, we'll have to see how she would behave in a riding therapy situation. I don't want to wait until the girl is actually here to figure that out. You can understand that, right?"

June nodded. What Ines was saying made sense. All along she had thought that riding therapy wouldn't be quite as simple as Marty wanted to believe.

"It would be a big help," Ines continued, "if we could try the whole thing with you as our guinea pig. Would you be willing to do that for me?"

"Of course, as long as you tell me what it is that I need to do."

"Oh, that's easy," said Ines. "You just have to pretend

that you are this girl. Your mother and I will lift you onto Modena's back and then I'll lead Modena around a bit and we'll see how she reacts."

"That's a terrific idea," exclaimed Marty. "Then you'll see that Modena will make a perfect therapy horse. Should I saddle her up?"

"A surcingle with handles would be better," said Ines. "Do you have something like that?"

"Of course. I'll be right back."

Marty ran into the stable and quickly returned with a surcingle, snaffle and lunge line.

"Ready to go."

Before long, she led the bridled horse to the sandy area behind the house. Ines and June followed a few yards behind her.

"This really is a lovely farm," said Ines and looked around with admiration. "Have you lived here long?"

"Not quite two years," answered June. "We moved here after my parents split up."

"Oh." Ines looked at her sympathetically. "I'm sorry."

"It's okay," said June. She didn't like to talk about the fact that her parents were divorced and quickly changed the subject. "Do you have a horse?"

"No." Ines suddenly looked quite sad. "I had a Haflinger mare, but I had to put her down last year. She was very old."

June swallowed. How horrible it must be to lose your horse, she thought.

"We have Haflingers, too," she said.

"Oh really?"

Ines suddenly looked extremely interested.

"Where are they?"

June pointed to the big paddock next to the sandy area.

"They're standing way in the back near the edge of the woods, you see? If you'd like, I can show them to you later."

"That would be great," said Ines. "Haflingers are really great horses, don't you think?"

"Let's say, they're very special horses. At least when you're talking about our Haflinger Gang."

"Haflinger Gang?"

"That's what we call them because they're always coming up with a new bit of mischief. Especially Navajo, their ringleader. He's a sly fellow. Our neighbor even wanted to sue us because they were constantly breaking loose and running through his fields."

"Haflingers are very clever animals," said Ines. "At any rate, it would make me really happy if you'd introduce me to your Haflinger Gang later."

By this time they had reached the spot where Marty was waiting for them with Modena.

Chapter 5

"Alrighty then," said Ines and looked around. Her gaze landed on a plastic chair at the edge of the mounting area.

"Okay, June, I'd like you to sit down on this."

June did as she was told, and Ines asked Marty to steady Modena next to the chair while Ines tried to help June up.

"June, don't try to stand up yourself," Ines warned her. "Pretend that you can't move your legs at all and need to be helped."

June tried to imagine it, but had to keep stopping herself from using her legs while she was being helped up. It was a pretty strange situation and she kept thinking about the girl whose place she was taking now. What must it be like to have to wait for others to help you all the time? Probably not very nice at all.

While Ines tried to help June onto Modena's back, Marty had her hands full trying to keep her horse still. The mare kept moving aside so that Ines and June even lost their balance once. They would have fallen down if June hadn't quickly used her legs to steady herself.

"Hmm," Ines said after a while. She wiped the sweat from her forehead. "As you can see, it really isn't all that easy. We've been at this for half an hour and June still isn't sitting on the horse."

"I just don't understand what has gotten into Modena," said Marty. "She never fidgets around like this."

June was surprised to see that the mare was sweating from all her agitation.

"I don't want to sound like a pessimist, but I don't think she's going to work out as a therapy horse," said Ines. "She doesn't have the right temperament for this stuff; she's much too sensitive. Standing still for such a long time is no good for her and she is just too nervous. Frankly, I don't see how I'll ever get June on her back."

"But what if we train her?" Marty asked pitifully. "We have almost a whole week."

Ines shook her head.

"No, that's too big a risk. We'd have to train anyway, but if she's already this nervous, then I'm afraid it's no use. As I said, she's much too sensitive. She's a sport horse. And she's too big."

"Now what will we do?!"

Marty sighed loudly and dropped down into the chair so quickly that she almost tipped over backwards.

"Well, take a look over there," said Ines. "It looks like we have an audience."

She pointed to the fence where the Haflingers had congregated and were watching them with big eyes.

"Aren't they sweet?"

Ines marched across the ring and June hurried to keep up with her.

"That's our Haflinger Gang. If there's something happening, then they're always in the front row to see it. They don't miss a thing."

Ines stroked the soft horse noses and ran her fingers through their thick platinum blonde manes.

"What is this one like?"

She pointed to the gelding in the middle of the group.

"That one is Navajo, the one I told you about. Their leader."

"Ah, so you're the one."

Ines brushed Navajo's thick forelock to the side and looked into his eyes.

"What about this horse?"

"What are you talking about?" June asked with astonishment.

"He does belong to you, doesn't he?"

"Yes."

June still didn't understand.

"I wonder if you could bring him to me."

"Now?"

"Yes, since I'm already here, why not now?"

"Yes, er, well, shouldn't we continue working with

Modena? I'm sure Mom will let you ride Navajo later on if you really want to, but I think we should take care of things with Modena first."

"Who said anything about riding?" Ines asked and looked at June with big eyes.

"But why else do you want me to get Navajo?"

"So that we can try him out as a therapy horse, of course."

June couldn't believe her ears. Navajo as a therapy horse? Ines couldn't be serious about that.

Or could she?

"Now listen to me, June. Modena is a lovely horse, but she is not cut out to be a therapy horse. She is too sensitive and too big. What I need is a sturdy horse with steady nerves that isn't too tall. And this fellow here looks like he's got all that."

"If you say so," June acquiesced. "But does it absolutely have to be Navajo? We could try one of the other Haflingers. Except the little one back there. That one belongs to my friend. How about Nino, here? He's really very nice."

"No, I want that one. He seems to be to be exactly the right one."

Marty was at least as surprised by Ines's suggestion as June had been. In addition, she seemed to be offended that the mischievous Haflinger gelding would be preferred over her beloved Modena. Still, Ines insisted that Navajo be given a try, and before long the small powerful gelding was standing next to the plastic chair where June had taken her seat again.

"Okay, June, now lay your arm across my shoulders and let me lift you up."

Before anyone could say boo, June was sitting on Navajo, who hadn't moved one millimeter despite all the jostling from the less than gentle manner in which she was heaved on top of him.

"He did that just wonderfully," said Ines after she had taken June a few times around the ring. "I don't understand what you have against him."

Marty, who had been standing next to Navajo's head, looked askance at him.

"Yeah, yeah, first he acts cool as a cucumber, but then ..."

"Nonsense. Navajo is a natural."

Ines lovingly patted Navajo's neck. The little gelding stood as still as a statue, as though he had never done anything else in his life.

"Does this mean that we don't have to cancel on the girl?" Marty asked hopefully.

Ines looked from Marty to June to Navajo and then back to Marty.

"Well, if June is willing to practice a little more with Navajo and me during the coming week, then I'd say we're good to go."

"What a relief!" Marty beamed. "I was so afraid that it wouldn't work out. But who would have thought that of all our horses Navajo would be the one to make it possible?" She scritched Navajo behind his short ears. "Could I have been so mistaken about you?"

"Let's wait and see," June mumbled. "Maybe something else will occur to him."

"Don't always be so negative, June," Marty reprimanded her. "You heard yourself what Ines said about him, and she should know. Anyway ..."

Before she could finish her thought, the phone in her jacket pocket rang. Marty dug it out and answered.

"Hello, it's Marty Sunshyne."

"Oh, Mrs. Schultz, how nice of you to call. What can I do for you?"

June listened closely, because it was extremely unusual for Vanessa Schultz to call Sunshine Farm. Was something wrong with Charly?"

"Pardon me?"

June watched a strange expression cross her mother's face.

"Oh really? Oh. Yes. Well, that is really very, uh, nice of you, er ..."

Marty walked off so that June couldn't hear any more of her conversation with Charly's mother. Instead she and Ines brought Navajo to the stable together and removed the snaffle and lunge line.

"What was it that gave you the idea to give Navajo a try?" said June as she pulled the halter over Navajo's head.

"All I needed was to look at his face," said Ines as she gingerly picked a hay straw out of his thick mane that had been overlooked when they curried him.

"Do you see how broad and flat his forehead is?"

June looked over Navajo's forehead with surprise and nodded.

"Yes, but what does that mean?"

"It suggests that he is a very balanced, friendly and reliable horse. And that impression is emphasized by the forelock right between his eyes."

"Really?" June asked skeptically. Navajo was friendly, but balanced and reliable? She wasn't too sure about that.

"And do you see his Roman nose? That is the sign of a self confident horse, one that knows what it wants."

June nodded. Anyone who ever had anything to do with the mischievous gelding would surely agree that Navajo had plenty of self-confidence and knew what he wanted.

"You can discover a lot about a horse's personality just by looking closely at his head. And with Navajo here, everything suggests that he will make a perfect therapy horse."

June swallowed. On the one hand, she didn't want to contradict Ines and be a killjoy for her mother's plans, but on the other hand, she felt Ines needed to know the truth. "I have to be honest with you. Navajo isn't exactly easy to handle. He really only does what he feels like doing."

"Nonsense!" said Ines contemptuously. "Navajo is a very intelligent horse and he wants to have a mission. It's important for him to understand that he's needed."

June looked skeptically at the Haflinger, whose eyes glinted mischievously from beneath his thick forelock. She hoped that Ines was right.

"June, you're not going to believe this…"

Marty was out of breath from running across the courtyard. She leaned on her elbows against the hitching post.

"That was Vanessa Schultz."

"I know," June said impatiently. "Did something happen to Charly?"

"No, we didn't talk about Charly. We talked about the fact that we still don't have someone who can do the cooking for us." She looked at Ines. "Can you cook, Ines?"

Ines shook her head.

"No, I can give therapeutic riding lessons, lead trail rides, muck out the stable, anything really – but I can't cook. Unless of course you'd like frozen dinners seven days a week."

"I thought as much," said Marty, exasperated. "Then I guess that means we'll have to take Mrs. Schultz up on her offer."

"What are you talking about, Mom?" June asked impatiently. "What kind of an offer? Does Mrs. Schultz know someone who can cook for us?"

Marty nodded. "You could say that."

"Come on, Mom, cut the suspense. Who does she have in mind?"

"Herself."

There was a long pause.

"Vanessa ... Schultz ... wants ... to ... cook ... for ... us?" June finally asked, very slowly, as though she couldn't believe her ears.

40

Marty nodded. "She said that she was taking the week off and would be coming out here with Charly. And that's not everything."

"Not everything? What else could there be?" asked June.

"She wants to bring her horse so that she can ride out here during the week."

"Summer Dream?" June asked incredulously. "Out here to Sunshine Farm? Where do you plan to board him?"

On one of the few occasions that she had visited her friend in Washington, DC, June accompanied Charly and her mother to the expensive stable where Mrs. Schultz boarded her horse. Summer Dream was a sinfully expensive, elegant Hanoverian mare that was trained to Grand Prix level dressage. Mrs. Schultz had received the horse as a birthday present from Charly's father. Presents like that were peanuts for a wealthy management consultant like him.

"Summer Dream probably hasn't stood freely on a paddock since she was a foal," said June. "In Washington she was either in her box or wrapped up tightly in a small corner of a paddock. What would you do if she injured herself? And where do you plan to keep her?"

Marty looked at June, downcast.

"Don't you think I know all that? But I couldn't exactly turn her down. We'll board Summer Dream in our emergency box and just keep our fingers crossed that none of the other horses get sick while she's here. We can also fence in a section of the paddock and then all we can do is hope that nothing happens to the animal. It really makes me uneasy that Mrs. Schultz wants to board such a valuable horse here. If only Bea didn't have to go and get chicken pox!"

"Well this'll be interesting," groaned June. "Vanessa Schultz is going to be our cook and she's bringing her valuable horse Summer Dream to Sunshine Farm. And Navajo will be our therapy horse. Can this possibly turn out well?"

Chapter 6

"I think I see it up ahead."

Mrs. Hendricks pointed to the farm at the top of the hill.

"That must be Sunshine Farm."

April squinted to see better in the bright sunlight. The car zipped along with fields and meadows on either side of them as they drove to the top of the hill. The buildings at Sunshine Farm formed a horseshoe. An ancient chestnut tree stood in the middle of the gravel courtyard. Underneath it stood a wooden table and long bench, where a boy was sitting and reading. When he noticed them coming, he set aside his book and walked over. April thought that he looked really nice, with his freckles and friendly smile.

"Hi, I'm Ben. Mrs. Sunshyne asked me to wait for

you because she had to take care of something in town quickly. You must be April, right?"

He reached out his hand to her. April looked at him, confused. How did he know her name? But then her face took on a darker expression when she heard her mother take her wheelchair out of the back of the car. How stupid of her. As if there were more girls coming who couldn't walk.

"Would you like me to help you?" Ben asked and stretched out his arm to her.

"No thanks," April mumbled. "I can manage by myself."

With great effort she swung herself into the wheelchair using both her arms. She tried not to let the strain show. All the while she asked herself if maybe she had made a mistake in coming here. All alone. But then she heard a horse neighing and slowly began to relax. No, it hadn't been a mistake to come here. The other kids didn't matter to her at all, as long as she could be around horses again! She turned around in the direction from which the neighing came and spied a beautiful white horse looking inquisitively in their direction.

"Oh, he's just beautiful," she breathed. "May I stroke him?"

"Of course," said Ben. "If you'd like, I can push you over there." When he noticed April's dark expression, he quickly added, "It's not so easy on the gravel, you know."

April looked around and sighed. Ben was right. She'd never be able to drive over the gravel by herself. Which meant that for this entire week she'd be dependent on help from others to get around. What was that going to be like?

As if he had read her mind, Ben said, "Mrs. Sunshyne asked me to assist you this week. If you have any questions or need something, then just let me know, okay?"

April's expression turned darker still, but then she looked into Ben's friendly face. He really did seem nice and he seemed to be sincere.

"All right," she said quietly. "Now can we go over to that horse? He's just beautiful."

"I, er, will take the bags out of the car," said Mrs. Hendricks, who was clearly relieved that her daughter had accepted Ben's offer. "Where can I put them?"

Ben indicated a small, bright building off on the side where the door was standing open. "Right in there, the first door on the right. That's where the girls sleep. April has the lower bunk right next to the door."

While Mrs. Hendricks unloaded the luggage, Ben pushed April over to the paddock where the white horse waited for her. He stretched his head over the fence and gave a friendly sniff to her outstretched hand.

"Wow," April whispered. "What a fantastic horse. Is this one of the horses you use for lessons?"

Ben shook his head and smiled.

"Oh my, you should be glad that June wasn't around to hear that. Just thinking about her Nelson giving lessons to someone else would probably give her a rash."

"June?"

April looked blankly at Ben.

"June Sunshyne, Mrs. Sunshyne's daughter. Actually

her name is Juniper, but no one ever calls her that. Nelson is her horse."

"So your name is Nelson," said April, and gently stroked the white horse's flared nostrils.

"He's an Anglo-Arabian," Ben explained, "and June rides jumping parcours with him. She loves warmbloods. But if you ask me, I think they're always too nervous. I prefer robust horses like Björn. He's a genuine Icelandic."

He pointed to the little gelding with the shaggy mane that was just ambling over to them at the fence.

"He's sweet," said April, although her gaze kept wandering back to Nelson. "I like warmbloods a lot, too."

"Have you ridden horses before?" Ben asked, surprised.

April looked down at the tops of her feet and nodded.

"I used to ride, yes. But that's something I'd rather not talk about."

"Okay, no problem," said Ben quickly. "Would you like to see the horse that you'll be riding?"

"Gladly. Where is it?"

"We need to go to a different paddock. The Haflinger Gang is on the other side."

"A Haflinger?" April said and tried to hide the disappointment in her voice. "Will I be riding a Haflinger?"

Ben nodded and motioned toward the powerful little gelding that was standing under an apple tree, grazing.

"There he is. His name is Navajo. Navajo, come on over here."

The Haflinger raised his head when he heard his name

and slowly walked over to the fence where they were waiting.

"Well, what do you think of him?" Ben asked. "Isn't he sweet?"

"Mm hmm," said April and brushed his thick forelock out of his face. He really was very sweet, but he was also very different from the white horse that she liked so much. And completely different from Bonaparte. April swallowed and felt the tears shoot into her eyes. But she couldn't cry now!

"Are you okay?" Ben was concerned. "Are you feeling sick?"

"No," April grunted and cleared her throat. "I'm just a little tired. Do you think you could show me where I'll be staying?"

"Sure," said Ben and he turned the wheelchair in the direction of the smaller building into which Mrs. Hendricks had disappeared with April's things. When they reached the old chestnut tree, a dark blue BMW with tinted windows pulled up onto the driveway.

"Is that Mrs. Sunshyne?" April asked.

"No," Ben laughed. "Mrs. Sunshyne definitely doesn't drive a BMW. I think that must be Charly and her mother. Charly is June's friend. She owns the little Haflinger that you may have noticed back there. Charly's father is part owner of Sunshine Farm, by the way, and her mother will be staying here this week to cook for the guests." Ben smiled conspiratorially. "Mrs. Sunshyne is incredibly good with horses, but she can't cook a thing."

"Hey, Ben!"

A girl with short, dark hair walked over to them while the woman struggled with the contents of the trunk of her car.

"Hi, Ben! How are you doing?"

"Hi, Charly. Can I introduce April to you? April, this is Charly."

"June and April," Charly laughed. "If this keeps up, pretty soon we'll have an entire calendar." She looked over her shoulder back to her mother, who was still taking bags and suitcases out of the trunk.

"Good grief, Mom, aren't you almost done with that?" she called.

Mrs. Schultz paused for a moment and then shook her head. April noticed that she was dressed in elegant, expensive clothes, while her daughter simply wore washed out jeans and beat up sneakers.

"Hey, wasn't your Mom going to bring along her horse?" asked Ben.

"Oh, Summer Dream will be right here. A caretaker from her riding stable is bringing her. My mother would never attach a horse trailer to her fancy car. See over there – there he is now!"

A jeep with a horse trailer behind it drove around the corner and stopped directly behind Mrs. Schultz's BMW.

"Oh, Summer is here!"

Mrs. Schultz put her bags down on the ground and walked to the door at the front side of the trailer. She opened it and peaked in.

"Summer, sweetie, how are you doing in there?"

"This will be like an adventure in the wilderness for Summer," Charly whispered and winked conspiratorially to April. "She happens to be a genuine dressage stable horse, you know. I'll bet she hasn't seen a real paddock in an eternity."

A man got out of the jeep and opened the back hatch of the trailer. Mrs. Schultz wasn't about to allow anyone else to lead her mare down the ramp and she personally guided her horse out of the trailer. April held her breath as the dark chestnut mare walked out of the trailer backwards and then surveyed the courtyard with her head held high. A shrill whinny shook her entire body. Or at least the part of her body that was visible. The mare was wearing a blanket and four thick tendon boots for the transport. But the part of her that was visible was enough for April. Summer was, by a very large margin, the most beautiful horse she had ever seen.

"Charly, do you know where I can take her?" Mrs. Schultz asked as she skillfully avoided Summer's hooves. The mare was exceedingly nervous and didn't stand still for a minute. Charly looked questioningly at Ben.

"You stay here with April," he said. "Then I'll show your mother the box where she can bring Summer."

"Does that horse really belong to you?" April asked breathlessly, still overwhelmed by the sight of the horse. "It is gorgeous."

"Yes, Summer really is beautiful. But to be honest, she's just too jittery for me. She gets all worked up over every little thing. My mother always used to want me to ride her, but I never felt like it. I much prefer my chubby little Haflinger. There's nothing that'll get him riled up," said Charly.

April could hardly believe what Charly had just said. Her mother owned the most incredible horse she had even seen and Charly would rather ride a Haflinger? Sometimes life really was unfair!

Chapter 7

By the time June and her mother returned from their errands, several cars were parked in the courtyard.

"See over there?" said June, pointing at the dark blue BMW with the tinted windows. "That looks like the new car Charly's mother just got. And there's a horse trailer, too. I wonder how Summer is behaving in this unfamiliar environment."

As if in answer to June's musings, a shrill whinny echoed across the courtyard as June and Marty opened their car doors. They looked at each other and then strode quickly across the courtyard to the emergency box. The upper door was open. A few kids whom June assumed to be camp guests were standing in front of it.

"Wow," said a girl with long blonde hair and glasses. "That horse is crazy."

June wasn't quite sure how she meant "crazy," but she did have to agree with the girl in every sense of the word. Just at that moment, Summer stuck her regal head with its narrow white blaze out of the open box door and let out a whinny that was loud – and crazy.

"Oh Summer, why don't you just relax!" a voice said from inside the box. "At this rate I'll never get your tendon boots off."

Summer took a few steps back and began to wildly turn in circles. Marty and June squeezed past the kids to the box and discovered Mrs. Schulz, who was trying to hold Summer's lead with one hand while attempting to take off the tendon boots with the other. She wasn't quite successful doing either because the mare simply refused to stand still and kept poking her head out of the door excitedly.

"Just a sec," said Marty and slipped through the box door. "I'll give you a hand."

Mrs. Schulz, who had only just noticed them, looked at them gratefully.

"Thanks, that would be a big help. Summer is all worked up and won't stand still. She needs to get used to her new surroundings first."

Marty nodded and took the lead from Mrs. Schulz's outstretched hand.

"I think it'll work best if you hold her and I take off the tendon boots."

Marty tugged gently on the lead and spoke to Summer Dream in calming tones. The mare continued to flare her nostrils excitedly, but she stopped turning in circles.

"Did you want to leave the blanket on her?" Marty asked after Mrs. Schulz had finally removed all four tendon boots. "It's pretty warm today."

Mrs. Schulz looked at her as if she had just spoken in Chinese. "Of course I'll leave the blanket on her," she said finally. "Summer is clipped; without the blanket she could catch a cold."

"Oh," said Marty as she removed the lead from the halter. "Then we'll leave the blanket on. No problem. We'll do all we can to ensure that Summer Dream is comfortable here this week, isn't that right, June?"

June nodded and looked at Summer Dream skeptically. They could surely give it a try, but she doubted that they'd have much success. The mare looked anything but happy in her new surroundings. Besides, in June's opinion a highly trained competition horse didn't belong at Sunshine Farm, which was something that could be said of Summer Dream's owner as well. With her light brown leather boots, the designer jeans and the stylish riding jacket, Vanessa Schulz looked more like she was on her way to go shopping at D.C.'s fanciest boutiques than about to spend a week at a riding camp for kids. The fact that the well-dressed woman with the perfectly styled hair would be spending the next week cooking for the kids was even more incomprehensible!

Marty didn't seem to notice any of this and said to Mrs. Schulz that it was "very friendly" of her to help them out this week.

"I'm so happy to do it," said Mrs. Schulz as she brushed a piece of hay off her jeans. "Charly so loves coming out to Sunshine Farm and I'm happy that I was able to join her this time. I've always wanted to go on a trail ride with her."

June was so blown away by this statement that her jaw dropped open. Mrs. Schulz wanted to go on a trail ride with Charly – on Summer Dream? The mare honestly didn't look like the kind of horse that would enjoy a relaxed trail ride.

"Er, Summer Dream needs to get acclimatized here first, don't you think?"

The mare was still whinnying and running around her box. June wondered if the mare would manage to get acclimatized at all during the course of the week.

"Now I'll show you your room and, uh, the kitchen of course. As I said, it's so friendly of you to help out this week. Show me where your bags are and I'll help carry them in."

"They're over there, next to the car," said Mrs. Schulz. June held her breath. If she didn't know better, she'd have thought that someone had mistakenly delivered a shipment of bags intended as inventory for a luggage store, considering how many suitcases there were.

"Is all that, er, I mean, er, is that your luggage there?" Marty stammered.

"Yes, and if I'm not mistaken, there should be a few more bags in the trunk," Mrs. Schulz said as she strode

over to her car. Marty was flabbergasted and stared after
her for moment, but then she shrugged her shoulders and
followed. June smiled. Vanessa Schulz was more or less
the exact opposite of her mother. She was curious to see
how the two women would get along during their week
together. But that wasn't her problem. She went off to
look for Charly, who she figured was with her Haflinger,
Nano. On the way to the paddock she ran into Ben who
was just showing two girls the way to the dairy kitchen.
That's what they called the building with the guest rooms
for the campers.

"Hi, June. This is Nellie and Sabrina. And this is
June. She's Mrs. Sunshyne's daughter and lives here at
Sunshine Farm."

"Really?" asked the girl named Nellie. She had red curls,
almost as many freckles as Ben and looked like she was a
lot of fun. "You live here? That must be totally cool."

"Do you have your own horse?" asked Sabrina. She
was the blonde girl with glasses whom June had noticed
earlier in front of Summer's box.

"Yes, the white horse that's standing over there at the
fence. His name is Nelson."

"Wow," said Sabrina. "He's really pretty. Almost as
pretty as that chestnut mare in the box. Is that horse also
for lessons?"

"The chestnut mare?" laughed June. "No, she's just
here for the week because her owner is helping my mom
with the cooking."

"Aww, that's too bad."

Sabrina pushed up her glasses and made a face.

"I was already hoping I could take care of her."

June bit her lip to keep from laughing. Vanessa Schulz's regal Summer Dream for lessons – now that was a crazy thought!

Chapter 8

Although June wanted nothing more than to keep looking for Charly, the fact that Marty was obviously still upstairs with Mrs. Schulz meant that she and Ben would have to take care of the guests. Two boys, who couldn't be more than ten years old, ran over the graveled courtyard and slid to a stop in front of her.

"Do you work here?"

They didn't wait for an answer.

"Where are the horses? We want to go for a ride, now."

"First of all, I don't work here, I live here," June observed. "And we won't be riding until this afternoon, after my mother assigns the horses to you. Anyway, my name's June, and this is Ben. What are your names?"

The boys introduced themselves as Mike and Sven

58

and they seemed to be quite nice – although as far as June was concerned, they were a little too spirited.

"And what are we supposed to do until then?" asked Mike with disappointment in his voice. "It's totally boring to just hang around and wait."

"Why don't you take a look around?" Ben suggested. "I'll bet you'll discover all kinds of things here."

"Oh man, that's a great idea!" said Sven and clapped Mike so hard on the shoulder that he stumbled forward a step. "Come on, buddy, let's go mix things up a bit!"

June watched them run off across the courtyard and disappear into the barn.

"Was it really a good idea to send them off by themselves?" she asked nervously. "Who knows what kind of trouble they'll get themselves into?"

"Oh, I wouldn't worry about them. Those two are just excited and they need to let off a little steam. After all, they are boys."

"I suppose you're speaking from personal experience?" June asked, laughing. "Anyway, we should keep an eye on them so that they don't tear the place apart."

"I'll take care of those two," said Ben.

"Don't you have enough to do already?" asked June. "Has she arrived yet?

"Yes, but she seemed a little tired and wanted to take a nap."

"And?"

"And what?"

"Is she nice?"

"I think so. She doesn't talk all that much, but that's no small wonder. I have to say I think it's really brave of her to come here all alone. It can't be easy for her," said Ben.

"Do you know why ...?"

Ben shook his head.

"No, I don't know why she's in a wheelchair. It seems to have been from some kind of accident, but I can't say what kind. She did say that she used to go riding and she really likes Nelson." He smiled. "But I think that she wasn't exactly thrilled about Navajo. Haflingers don't seem to be her cup of tea."

June rolled her eyes.

"The girl has taste. I just hope that she'll find a way to get along with him. But more than that, I hope our little rascal behaves and doesn't do anything too nutty."

"Oh come on, June, just relax," Ben warned. "You can't worry about every little thing all week long. First you're afraid that Mike and Sven will destroy the farm, now you're worried that Navajo will get into trouble."

June took a deep breath.

"A riding farm like this is a huge responsibility. It would be a catastrophe for Mom if something bad happened."

"While we're on that subject," said Ben, "where is your mother anyway? I haven't seen her at all today."

"Oh, she's upstairs with Mrs. Schulz. She's probably showing her the kitchen right now. Poor Mom. I think it's really awkward for her having Charly's mother here all week."

"Why? It's so nice of her to help you out."

"I know, it really is. But I get the feeling that Mom feels insecure around her. No wonder – she looks so stylish and together."

"Exactly the opposite of her daughter," said Ben and pointed to Charly who had just climbed through the fence of the Haflinger paddock and was on her way over to them.

"Hi, Charly!"

"Hi, June! I thought I'd never find you. Where have you been all this time?"

"I was running errands with Mom. We were out buying all the stuff your Mom needs for dinner. It's so nice of her to help us out and fill in for Bea."

"Oh," said Charly, "I think it's fun for her. She prepared for this week with military style precision. I think my Mom sees this as a sort of adventure vacation."

Once again a shrill whinny resounded across the courtyard.

"I think that goes for Summer Dream, too," said June. "The poor thing is beside herself."

Charly frowned and shook her head.

"To be honest, Summer is almost always beside herself. There's nothing that doesn't get her upset. You should have been there when we were loading her into the trailer; that was pretty crazy."

June had no trouble imagining what a difficult time they must have had if the huge mare didn't want to get into the trailer.

"Maybe it'll calm her down to come out of her box," June suggested. "Ben and I staked off a bit of the field behind the stable for her."

Charly shrugged her shoulders.

"Maybe. But I wouldn't take her out unless you've asked my mother first. She'll flip out if anything happens to her beloved horse."

Chapter 9

"Okay, is everyone here?"

Marty was leaning on the hitching post with a slip of paper in her hand. She looked out over the group. The new camp guests standing in front of her were all excited and on edge over which horse or pony would be theirs for the week.

"Okay, then let's start with April. Marty's gaze fell on April. "You'll have Navajo. Ines, who will be your riding instructor, is getting him ready. Ben will take you over to him in a minute."

June curiously observed the girl who was sitting quietly in her wheelchair. She nodded her head almost imperceptibly. Aside from that, she didn't show any emotion. How did she feel right now? Was she nervous? June sighed sympathetically and decided she would pay more attention to April.

While June was lost in thought, Marty continued to assign horses to riders. Alina, a shy girl with dark blonde hair, was an advanced rider. For that reason, Marty assigned her Prince Pepper, the Hanoverian gelding. June and her mother periodically rode him to keep him in form. He was one of the horses that Marty had bought for lessons after Charly's father became a partner in Sunshine Farm.

Mike got Doreen, the German Riding Pony mare, and Lars got Welcome. June thought that a fitting combination because both Lars and the brown gelding were incredibly big. Marie, on the other hand, got a chestnut mare named Fancy Girl.

"So, now I have three Haflingers to give out." Marty grinned. "Who is brave enough to take them on? These fellows are pretty crafty!"

The camp guests who hadn't yet been assigned a horse looked at each other and giggled nervously.

"Nellie, you get Ninja. Sabrina gets Nino. And Sven gets Noel."

That left one little girl who was staring at Marty with big round eyes and chewing on her lower lip.

"No need to worry, Elli." Marty smiled soothingly at her. "You get Flori. He's the little black pony with the shaggy mane. Maybe you've already noticed him?"

Obviously Elli had noticed the Shetland-mix, because a broad smile brightened her face.

"Okay, let's get going!" called Marty. "What are you waiting for? Go find your horses and get them ready so that our riding lesson can begin. June and I will help you."

64

As if a starting shot had been fired, everyone ran off. June and Marty had their hands full making sure that each guest got both the correct horse and the correct tack. When all the horses were finally curried and saddled, she went into the stable to get the lunge and the lunge whip.

The next part was one of June's favorite activities at Sunshine Farm. When her mother started the camp June hadn't had any idea how much fun giving riding lessons to beginners would be. She whistled a happy tune as she walked over to Elli, who had diligently curried Flori's thick black coat. Now she was brushing through the pony's unruly mane. Or at least she was trying to.

"You've done a good job, Elli," said June. "There's not much you can do about his mane. Flori's mane is almost as unmanageable as he is."

"Unmanageable? Are you saying he's wild?" Elli gave June a frightened look.

"Don't worry," June said soothingly. "Wild is the last word I'd use to describe Flori, but he can be pretty stubborn sometimes. Aside from that he's the sweetest pony you'll ever meet."

As if to emphasize what June had just said, the little Shetland mix gelding turned his head to the side and looked at the two girls with his huge dark eyes.

"Sometimes I think you understand every word I say," laughed June and lovingly scratched him behind his small fluffy ears. She grabbed the pony saddle that had been slung over the hitching post and laid it on Flori's back.

65

Next she firmly tightened the girth around the pony's round belly and then positioned the snaffle bit.

"And now we're about to get going," said June and received a grateful smile from Elli in return. The little girl was so excited that she stood next to Flori, shifting from foot to foot, impatiently waiting for the lesson to start. June took the halter off the small black pony, pulled the snaffle over his head and then pressed the reins into Elli's hand.

"Here, you lead him to the ring."

Elli had so much fun leading him, even if Flori did stop at every patch of grass to bend his head down and try to eat. June had to step in a few times along the way until they finally reached the ring where the others were already waiting.

On the way, she noticed Ben and Ines off in a corner by themselves, working to get Navajo ready while April observed them from where she was sitting in her wheelchair. She couldn't help but feel sympathy for the girl. It must be terrible not to be able to do anything yourself and be dependent on others for help.

In the ring, she helped Elli onto Flori's back and led the little gelding in a few rounds of walking. At the same time, Ines walked over to the ring with Navajo. She stopped at the entrance to the ring. June was curious. During their practice rounds over the last few days, the small, powerful gelding had been very well behaved. Still June was surprised to see how quietly and patiently he stood there now, waiting until Ines helped April onto his back. June would have loved to continue observing them, but for now she had to take care of Elli and Flori. She attached the bearing rein to the snaffle rings and checked that the girth was pulled tightly enough.

"Okay, Elli," she said when she finished. "Take your feet out of the stirrups. Now you can lay your head down onto Flori's neck and give him a big, strong hug."

Elli looked at her uncertainly, but did as she was told. "Now close your eyes," June told her, "and you'll get a better feel for him. Well? How do you like that?"

"It's great," Elli whispered, her eyes shut tight. "He's so warm and he smells so good."

"Yes," said June. "That's what I always think, too."

"Do you ride Flori, too?"

Elli was sitting upright in the saddle again, looking at June inquisitively.

"No," laughed June. "I'm much too big for him. But sometimes I do that on my own horse. On Nelson. And every time I do it, I think about how incredibly good it feels."

Elli nodded enthusiastically and tried it again.

"Why don't we take him for a walk again?" June asked after a few moments. "Otherwise Flori will fall asleep in place if he just stands around." Carefully she led the pony to start him up, walking at a leisurely pace. "We'll let him walk at this pace for a few minutes so that you can get used to his movements. Just relax; Flori is a good fellow."

With Flori walking around the ring, June had a few

minutes to look around. The other riders had shortened their reins and were trotting.

In the meantime, Ines led Navajo to walk on the second track. She said something to April that June couldn't make out because they were too far apart, but June noticed that April seemed tense and was holding onto both grips of the surcingle very tightly.

Elli clearly felt at ease on Flori's back and June taught her a few more exercises to make her more flexible in the saddle. After the little girl had completed them to her satisfaction, June brought the Shetland mix to a stop and explained about trotting and posting to Elli. Because finding and maintaining the right rhythm wasn't all that easy, Elli had to first practice a little standing in place. It was a strenuous exercise for the girl, and her face turned red and she started sweating. Once Elli was relatively confident with the movements, June gave the command to begin trotting. Flori didn't need to be asked twice and happily began trotting.

"Okay Elli, when I say one, then you stand up, and when I say two, you sit down again. Got it? Alright then. One – two – one – two."

Elli panted from exertion, but kept up quite well, considering that she has just started learning to ride. Just as she started to run out of steam, June slowed Flori down to a walk.

"That was just terrific," June praised her enthusiastically. "Now you can take a little break and then we'll try it again."

"Yes, please!" Elli called out and wrapped both her arms around Flori's short, thick neck. "Flori is soooo sweet. He's the best pony in the whole world."

The little black pony turned one ear back toward them and snorted with satisfaction.

"I'm sure he understood everything you just said," laughed June. "Don't exaggerate though, otherwise he might think he's something special."

"But he is something special," said Elli. She sat up again and straightened out her riding helmet. "Can we do some more?"

June could hardly keep from smiling. Seeing Elli now reminded her of when she was still a little girl and desperately wanted to learn all there was to know about riding as quickly as possible. Back then she thought there was nothing nicer in the world than sitting on the back of a horse or pony – she still felt that way today. Then again, that didn't apply to just any horse or pony, June thought as she suddenly noticed Ninja taking a huge step forward. Nellie was holding on to his light colored mane as tightly as possible to keep from being thrown out of the saddle. Those darn Haflingers! June bit her lower lip and shortened the lunge to keep Flori nearer to herself. It was obvious that the Haflingers were about to start acting up again.

Nellie slowed Ninja down to a walk and adjusted her posture in the saddle.

"Once you've managed to collect yourself, I'd like you to begin trotting again," Marty called out to her. June noticed that her mother's voice sounded quite annoyed. No small wonder, when she thought about how many riding lessons had been reduced to utter chaos by the Haflinger Gang.

Nellie shortened the reins and pressed her heels into his sides – and then it happened. Ninja changed direction so suddenly that Nellie slid off the saddle and found herself sitting on his neck. The small powerful gelding took a step to the side and then galloped off in long strides. Nellie didn't have a chance. After a few strides she began to lose her grip and slid sideways down Ninja's shoulder. Before Marty could reach her, Noel and Nino began to buck and then chase after Ninja. Sabrina reacted just in time and was able to hold on to Nino's long mane. But it came as such a surprise to Sven that he plopped down onto the sand just like Nellie. June stood next to Flori and breathlessly observed the spectacle that was taking place before her eyes. Suddenly it wasn't just the Haflingers that were flipping out, but the entire group! Even Welcome, who was normally so even-tempered, galloped off in powerful strides and resisted any effort to slow him down. June didn't know in which direction to look.

Slowly, though, the horses calmed down one after the other and the situation in the ring returned to normal. In the meantime Ben had rounded up the two riderless Haflingers and brought them back to Nellie and Sven. June was flabbergasted. What confusion! And all of it because of the Haflinger Gang. But wait a second – this time it wasn't all of the Haflingers. She was surprised to discover that Navajo was quiet and peaceful as a lamb, standing outside the ring with Ines. He didn't even seem to be interested in all the chaos. This time the Haflingers didn't even need their leader in order to bring on the chaos. Nellie and Sven mounted their horses again and for the rest of the lesson they were the best-behaved horses in the world ...

Chapter 10

With her eyes round as saucers, April watched the horses
chase each other around the ring. What a relief that
Navajo had stayed so calm. She didn't dare to think about
what she would have done if he had bolted, too. Nothing,
she thought darkly. She wouldn't have done anything at
all. How could someone who couldn't even move her
legs? As it was, she felt so miserably insecure, as if she
had never sat upon a horse in her entire life. When she
thought more about it, she realized it was actually true
in a sense, because the April who rode horses back then
didn't exist anymore.

"April?"

April flinched and looked at Ines, who was looking up
at her.

"Didn't you hear me?"

"I, er, no. I suppose I was, um, deep in thought," April stammered. She didn't want to let on what she had been thinking about.

"I said, let's get going again now, okay?"

No! April would've liked to shout out loudly. No! No! No! But she didn't want to show any vulnerability in front of the stocky little woman with the friendly face. She was finally here and she would just have to press on.

Ines led Navajo back into the ring and began to walk with him on the second track. April held on to the grips of the surcingle so tightly that her knuckles went white.

"Okay, you should be accustomed to Navajo's gait by now," said Ines. "Now why don't you let go of the belt and lay your hands loosely on top of your thighs." Carefully April released her grip but then grabbed onto the belt again immediately.

"No problem," said Ines. "We've got time. Let's start with one hand first. Let go with your left hand and lay it on your leg."

Reluctantly, April let go and did as Ines had asked.

"Okay, that's very good," Ines praised her. "Now you just have to loosen up a little. You're still very tense. Try to relax."

April looked over at the little girl riding on the black pony led on the lunge. The girl was so cheerful and was really doing a good job. She could remember when she was that age and had started riding. Today it seemed to her as if it had happened in another life.

"That wasn't so bad, was it?" asked Ines after they had

completed a round. "And now I'd like you to do the same thing with your right hand.

Reluctantly April released her right hand from the surcingle and laid it on her leg. Although she wasn't ready to admit it to herself, she did notice that it was somewhat easier this time than it was on her first try. Ines had also noticed.

"You see? You just have to be able to let go, and then it isn't nearly as difficult any more. The less you tense up, the easier it is."

April pressed her lips together until her mouth looked like little more than a thin line on her face. Easy was the last word she would use to describe what she was doing. She jealously looked over at the others who were now galloping through their section of the ring while she was barely able to manage riding in a walk while holding on with one hand.

"What do you think?" Ines asked. She stood still and looked over at her. "Would you like to give it a try with both hands off?"

April shook her head emphatically.

"No. I think that was enough for today. I'm exhausted."

"Oh." Ines looked ashamed. "I'm really very sorry. I didn't want to overwork you."

"It's not your fault," said April. "I just get ... tired quickly."

She lowered her head to avoid Ines's scrutinizing gaze. She would feel humiliated if her riding instructor realized that she wasn't telling the truth. Of course she wasn't tired, she just didn't feel like being led around the ring anymore while the others were able to ride around freely and have fun.

Ines led her out of the ring to where Ben was waiting with her wheelchair.

"Well?" he asked. "Did you like it?"

"Mm-hmm," was all April said. Without another word, she allowed herself to be helped into her wheelchair. Ben seemed to understand that she didn't feel like talking about the riding lesson and silently wheeled her across the yard to the hitching area, where Ines was in the process of removing Navajo's leather surcingle. Ben handed April a currycomb.

"Here, I'm sure you'd like to groom Navajo a little before we take him back to the paddock."

Actually April had hoped that she could go directly back to her room, but when Navajo turned his head to her and looked at her from under the thick white forelock with that amused expression in his eyes, she haltingly took the currycomb. Why not, actually? After all, it wasn't the Haflinger's fault.

Just as she began currying his belly in gentle circling motions, June walked over to her.

"Hi," she said and stood next to April. "I haven't introduced myself yet. I'm June, Marty's daughter."

"I know, I've seen you around already," said April. "You have a very beautiful horse, in my opinion."

"Oh really?" June seemed pleased by the compliment. "Well, he's quite different from Navajo."

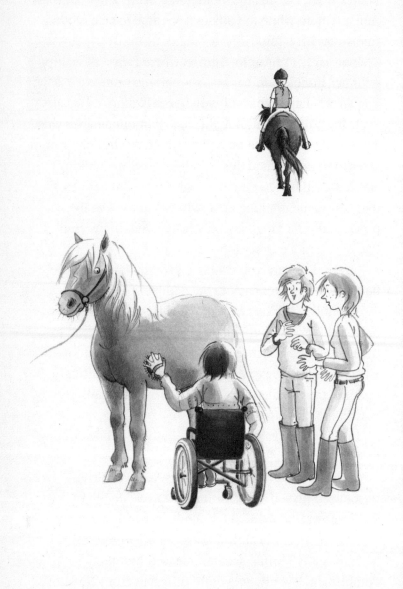

June smiled and ran her flat hand along Navajo's round belly. "Of course Navajo's really great," she added apologetically. "But I prefer the delicate, lively horses. Nelson is a pure Anglo-Arabian."

April almost told her that she felt the same way. That she also much preferred lively horses. Almost. Because then she remembered that this was part of a chapter that belonged to the distant past, a time in her life that was over forever.

Chapter 11

After all the excitement, June was famished and helped
everyone to finish up quickly and get back to the house.
Besides, she couldn't wait to find out what Mrs. Schultz,
with Charly's help, had made for lunch.

"Mmmm, that's smells really good!" said Mike as he
went into the kitchen.

"What are we having today?"

June shrugged her shoulders.

"No idea," she said, but she had to admit that it really
did smell delicious.

At the table, she sat down next to Charly and Ben
and stared with curiosity at the steaming pots on the
table.

"We're having chicken curry with rice," Charly
whispered, as if she had read June's thoughts.

June helped herself to a huge portion and closed her eyes as she savored the first bite.

"I had no idea that your mother could cook so well." She said.

"Oh, she's a really good cook. Unfortunately she usually doesn't have enough time to do much cooking because she's stuck in the office until late," said Charly with a trace of regret.

June looked at her sympathetically. Charly didn't have an easy time of it, even though her family was very well off. The problem wasn't just that her parents were divorced; on top of that her mother put in long hours working for a well-known marketing firm. As a result, Charly spent a lot of time on her own. Whenever she thought about it, June knew that she didn't want to trade places with her friend. Marty didn't have much money and couldn't cook to save her life, but at least she was always there for June and could take care of her if she needed help. Although she still had to get used to Mrs. Schultz's presence at Sunshine Farm, she was happy for Charly that she could spend all this time with her mother.

"What do you think?" she asked. "Why don't we take Summer up to the paddock after lunch?"

"Your mom already talked to my mother," answered Charly. "They decided that they'd wait until early tomorrow morning to try it, when it's nice and sunny. The way I know Summer, she's probably still far too agitated."

"But we can still go up to the ring, don't you think?"

June asked. She, Charly and Ben had decided that they would go for another ride together this afternoon after all the excitement had died down.

"Of course, I can hardly wait to finally go for a ride on Nano."

"It must be terrible for you, seeing him so infrequently, huh?"

"I really do miss him a lot. My mother even suggested to me that we board him at Summer's stable, but I'd rather not do that. I know that Nano would be totally depressed there, and I don't want to do that to him. Besides, just think how the people would stare if I were to show up with my little runt."

June had to laugh at the thought. At the stable in Washington, all the horses were of Summer's quality. An undersized fat-bellied Haflinger with a long mane would surely cause a commotion there.

"Besides, I really do prefer that he's here," said June. "If Nano were in Washington, then I wouldn't get to see you any more."

Charly let out a deep sigh.

"That would be rotten. I can't even imagine life without you and Sunshine Farm. Don't you agree that it's the most beautiful place in the world?"

"That's for sure." June smiled and shoveled another huge portion of chicken curry onto her plate. While she was chewing it with gusto, her gaze fell upon April, who sat silently at the other end of the table, not touching her food.

"Say, have you had a chance to talk to April yet?" she

asked in a quiet voice so that no one but Charly would hear. Her friend nodded. "Yes, I think she's very nice."

"She's so quiet," said June pensively. "If you ask me, she looks like she's not enjoying being here."

Charly swallowed a bite of her chicken curry and then shrugged her shoulders. "Maybe, but I don't think that's hard to understand. Everything here must be difficult for her, as the only person in a wheelchair. She probably feels lonely and left out. I can sympathize with her – that's pretty much how I felt my first time here."

Today June could hardly picture how incredibly unhappy Charly had been during her first visit to Sunshine Farm; so unhappy that she even wanted to run away.

She let out an even deeper sigh. "I wonder if we can help her?"

Charly wrinkled her forehead. "Hard to say. But one thing's for sure, whatever you do, don't show her that you feel sorry for her. I think that would bother her more than anything else, because it would make her feel even more like an outsider."

June looked at Charly. Was her friend speaking from experience? Charly had also been very withdrawn that first time at Sunshine Farm and didn't want to have anything to do with anyone else. At the end of the week, though, she didn't want to leave.

"Who knows?' June said finally. "Maybe tomorrow things will be better for her."

Chapter 12

When she heard the footsteps, April closed her eyes and pretended to be asleep. The girls in her room were nice, but she wanted to be alone and didn't want to have to talk to anyone else. The day had been strenuous enough already. And disappointing.

April herself was surprised by the realization, but she was disappointed. She had thought that all she needed to feel happy again was to be around horses, but it wasn't that simple. Everything was completely different from the way it used to be, back when she used to spend practically every day in the riding stable taking care of her foster horse, Bonaparte. To April that felt like an eternity ago, as if she had been a different person. But that's what she was now; a different person.

She had so admired June today on her spirited

Anglo-Arabian. Nelson was a beautiful horse and his owner rode him very well. They made a harmonious unit, just as things should be; the opposite of herself and the little Haflinger. Over the last few days she had so looked forward to sitting on a horse again. When it had finally happened, it was so different from how she had imagined it. Not just because she couldn't feel her legs. The movements were completely different from before. And then there was the feeling of helplessness, of being utterly dependent on the horse and the riding instructor, and that she couldn't do anything alone. She used to be a good rider and, like June, she loved jumping. She had even started in a few tournaments and brought home a ribbon here and there. What happened today was as if she had never been on a horse before in her life. Navajo and Ines couldn't help it and both of them had really tried hard this afternoon. But much to her disappointment, she had to conclude that riding couldn't give her what it once did. April took a deep breath and turned to lie with her face to the wall. She didn't want anyone to see the tears running down her cheeks. She thought about Bonaparte and tried to remember how she used to gallop through the fields with him. Oh, Bonaparte! If only she hadn't had the stupid idea to ride around the paddock with him! If she had only brought him straight to his box. If, if, if ... April put her face in her pillow and cried softly until sleep overtook her.

The next morning she waited to get out of bed until the other girls had left the room. She packed the things that had been carefully hung over the wheelchair that was standing next to her bed and began to get dressed. Just as she finished, the door opened and June slipped in to the room.

"Good morning," she said and came a few steps closer. "Did you sleep well?"

April nodded, "Yes, thanks."

June took another step closer to April and then sat down next to her on her bed.

"I'm supposed to tell you that we're about to have breakfast. If you're ready, then I can take you with me now. After that we have riding lessons. I just hope that the Haflingers behave a little better today. Er, the other Haflingers. Navajo was a model of good behavior yesterday. Did you know that Navajo used to be really mischievous and is actually the ringleader of the Haflinger Gang? He must think you're really special. Normally he would never sit out an opportunity like yesterday." June laughed out loud as she thought about all the tumult in the riding ring yesterday.

April forced herself to smile. She didn't want to admit how much the situation unnerved her yesterday. In the past she would have laughed about something like that, but yesterday she was afraid that her horse might bolt, too. What a stupid idea it had been to believe that everything could be like it used to be. Nothing would ever be the same again. Nothing.

"Are you okay, April?" June asked, with concern in her voice. "You look so gloomy."

"Huh?" April looked at her with astonishment. "Oh,

no, everything's just fine. I was just thinking about something else."

"Well, what do you say, shall we head out?" June asked and stood up without waiting for an answer. "Because I'm starved."

"Alright," said April jovially and let June help her into her wheelchair. Outside in the courtyard, she breathed in the fresh spring air. The mornings were still quite cool, but there wasn't a cloud in the sky and the sun was shining brightly. April looked around. Over at the paddock she saw Ben, who was pushing around a wheelbarrow filled with hay.

"See? The horses are getting their breakfasts before they go to work," giggled June.

"What's on the schedule for today?" April asked, just to have something to say.

"This morning we have riding lessons and then after lunch we'll go on a trail ride.

"I guess the trail ride doesn't apply to me," April said bitterly.

June was silent for a moment before she found her voice again. "Er, sorry about that, I, er, well some of us will go on a trail ride. But you and Elli will stay here and go for another round in the ring."

April groaned.

"Sounds pretty boring."

She didn't know herself why she had said that. It wasn't June's fault that she was in a wheelchair and couldn't ride normally any more. The opposite was true.

Everyone here was trying so hard to make her stay at Sunshine Farm as pleasant as possible.

"I'm sorry," she said contritely. "I didn't mean that the way it sounded, okay? It's just that everything ... isn't all that easy."

"I believe you," said June empathetically. "If you need help or want someone to talk to, then you can come to me, okay?"

A tiny smiled brightened April's face.

"It's a deal."

They had reached the door of the main house. June brought her into the kitchen where Marty and another woman were just setting the table. Yesterday she had been introduced as the cook, but April was amazed by how perfectly styled she was again this morning. This woman certainly didn't look like a cook.

"Oh, hello April," Marty greeted her and puffed a red curl out of her face. "Did you sleep well?"

April nodded and took a seat on the chair that Marty had positioned for her.

"Has June told you what we have planned for today?"

Before April could even answer, June butted into the conversation.

"I don't think it's all that exciting for April to go riding in the ring twice a day. It's a little boring, you know." She gave April a conspiratorial wink.

"Oh really?" Marty looked at them with an expression of surprise. "I understand what you mean, but ..."

"Don't worry on my account," said April darkly. "It's

perfectly clear to me that you can't go on a trail ride with someone like me. Really, nobody needs to show me any extra consideration."

April's words shocked Marty and her jaw dropped open.

"I, uh, well ... I mean ..." she stammered and gesticulated wildly with her hands.

April squirmed in her chair. She hated it when people around her got flustered because they thought they had said the wrong thing.

"Well, I have an idea," said June taking over the discussion again.

"Yes?" Marty looked at her daughter gratefully. "Then let us hear it."

"I have a feeling that Elli doesn't think it's too exciting to be lunged twice a day either. Not to mention how Flori feels. So I thought that Ines and Ben could take Elli and April for a walk on the horses. Ben would lead Flori and Ines would take Navajo."

Marty beamed happily.

"That sounds like a great idea, don't you think, April? That way everyone gets to go on a trail ride."

April clenched her teeth together tightly and tried not to break into tears. A simple walk on the horse, where she'd be led around like a little child. It couldn't possibly get any worse. But she didn't want to disappoint Marty and June, who seemed so pleased with their idea.

"Mm-hmm, that would be just great," she said quietly and quickly took a sip of her orange juice to keep herself from crying.

❖   ❖   ❖   ❖

In the meantime, the others had all arrived and noisily taken their places at the table. All of them had a hearty appetite, except for April, who could barely manage to choke down a piece of toast. After breakfast, they all went down to the courtyard to get their horses ready. Ines had already pulled into the courtyard with her noisy old yellow beetle and collected Navajo from the paddock.

The small powerful chestnut stretched his big head inquisitively toward April as Ben pushed her as close to him as possible. She stretched out her hand and stroked his soft nose. Navajo really was nice, even though he wasn't at all the kind of horse that April had expected. But from now on, the kind of horse April had expected was forever out of her reach. She sighed. Somehow she had to finish out this week and then that would be the end of riding for her. At least no one would be able to say that she hadn't given it one last try.

When Navajo was ready, Ines suggested that April mount him right then and there.

"He's so well-behaved that he'll surely stay still."

Despite her foul mood, April noticed that it was far easier to mount him today than it had been yesterday.

"You see?" asked Ines and smiled up at her. "It gets better every day. It's all just a question of practice."

She grabbed a lunge line from where it was lying under the hitching post and attached it to Navajo's left snaffle ring.

"What do think about trying to trot a little today?"

April swallowed and looked at Ines with fearful eyes. Yesterday they had walked, but the thought of a trot made her stomach feel queasy.

"We'll see how it goes," Ines tried to calm her. "No need to get stressed out, okay? I'll lead you around the ring first and then we can see how you feel. I just hope that the other horses behave a little better today."

Ines didn't need to worry. The Haflingers that had created all the commotion yesterday were completely different today. They trundled along like old teaching horses, not letting anything irritate them. On the other side of the ring, June lunged Elli and the small black pony. The little girl was doing well today with a light trot and was having a lot of fun riding. April's heart suddenly grew heavy.

"Well, April? How do you feel? Are you up for a little trotting?" asked Ines. "I think you are sitting very solidly, and Navajo is quite gentle."

Trotting! Thoughts were swirling through April's head. On the one hand, she was incredibly frightened to ride any faster than a walk. She still didn't feel completely confident on Navajo's back. On the other hand, she liked the idea of trotting, to feel the wind against her face. She was quiet for a moment and thought it over. Why not, really? Ines would surely be careful so that she didn't fall off. She opened her mouth in order to agree, but then shut it again and shook her head. No. Even if she didn't fall off, it still wouldn't be the same as before, when she was carefree and trotted and galloped across the fields.

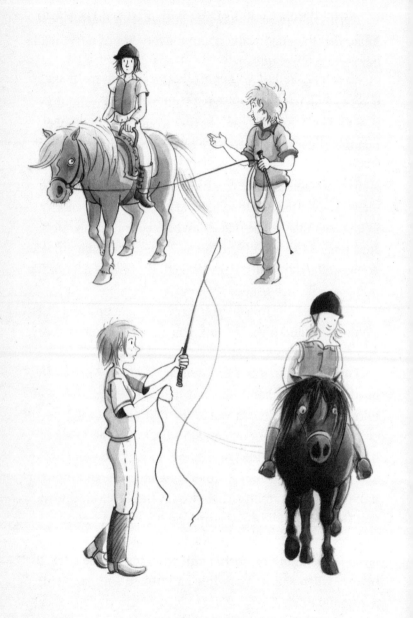

"No, I'd rather not, I'm um, very tired and I'd like to stop for now."

Ines looked at her with an expression of surprise.

"Really? Well, if you don't feel well, then we'll skip it. We can try it again tomorrow."

She led Navajo back to the hitching post and helped April down and into her wheelchair. Ben walked over to them.

"Hey, I thought you'd still be in the ring. Is anything wrong?" he asked with concern in his voice.

"April is tired and wanted to stop," said Ines. "It's best if you lie down for a rest, April, so that you'll feel up to going on our walk this afternoon."

Chapter 13

"Whew, that went really well today," Marty concluded with relief as the riding lesson came to an end and the campers took care of their horses. June, who was helping Elli to groom Flori, agreed.

"Today the Haflingers were really professional, like genuine teaching horses," she laughed.

"And Navajo is still behaving very well," added Marty with a smile. "You didn't expect that, did you?"

"Nope, not at all. But to be honest, he didn't have much time to misbehave today. Why did Ines wrap things up so early today?"

"Apparently April was still a bit tired," answered Marty. "No wonder, it must all be very strenuous for her."

"Tired?" June looked at her doubtfully. April hadn't said very much at the breakfast table, but she certainly didn't seem very tired. Could there be another reason? Hard to say, considering how close-mouthed April had been up until now. Maybe she didn't like it here? June decided that she had to talk to Ben about it, considering how well he and April seemed to get along.

"Marty?"

June turned around and held her breath. Mrs. Schultz was walking toward them wearing brown leather riding boots, dark brown riding pants and a beige-brown checkered jacket.

"Yes, er, Vanessa?"

June had to suppress a laugh. Her mother seemed to have a real problem with being on a first name basis with Mrs. Schultz. All in all, her mother seemed intimidated by the presence of Charly's mother, almost like a little girl.

"Lunch is ready now," Mrs. Schultz piped in. "And I'd like to use the time to give Summer a little exercise. Is the ring in use?"

"No one is using it right now," answered Marty and looked at Mrs. Schultz doubtfully. "Maybe you'd like to lunge her first? She's been in her box since yesterday afternoon and she's sure to be pretty worked up."

"No," Mrs. Schultz shook her head decisively. "Lunging is always so hard on the legs. I'd rather not take any chances."

June had already noticed that Mrs. Schultz didn't want to take any risks when it came to the legs of her beloved Summer. After Summer Dream had more or less calmed down yesterday, Mrs. Schultz had tightly bandaged up her legs again so that she wouldn't injure herself in any way. Summer Dream was a very, very expensive horse, and she needed special attention. But although June found the chestnut mare to be very beautiful, she had more praise for her beloved Nelson, who lived in the open stable from May through October. Then during the coldest months of the year he spent his days on the paddock and was only in his box at night. Without bandages or tendon boots.

"Then why don't you ask Charly to ride with you," Marty suggested. "June, go tell Charly that she should go for a ride with her mother."

June didn't have to look hard to find Charly. She was standing on the paddock with her Nano, massaging through the little Haflinger's thick mane. He was obviously enjoying the attention.

"Okay, Nano, let's get going," she said after June told her Marty wanted her to join her mother in the ring. "Then let's make sure that poor old Summer doesn't go totally nutty!"

By the time June returned to the courtyard with Charly and Nano, Mrs. Schultz had already taken Summer out of her box and tied her to the hitching post. The mare was dancing impatiently in place and whinnying shrilly. She refused to calm down even after Charly tied up Nano next to her. The undersized little Haflinger looked even smaller than usual next to the impressively large mare. He sniffed Summer inquisitively while the mare made loud noises and flattened back her ears.

"Charly, be careful that your pony doesn't injure her," said Mrs. Schultz reproachfully.

"Nano isn't a pony, he's a Haflinger," Charly retorted angrily. "And if anyone around here is going to get hurt, then it'll be Nano, by your Summer. She's acting like a bull in a china shop."

"Charly, please. I'll pretend I didn't hear that," said Mrs. Schultz, clearly offended. "Summer is just a little confused, that's all. You'll see; she'll be back to her old self in a little bit."

June and Marty smiled knowingly at each other. What they were just witnessing was a typical mother-daughter riding conflict. Situations like this happened all the time. There was no way around it when mother and daughter shared the same hobby.

Finally Summer and Nano were saddled and ready to go into the ring. Summer pranced about next to Mrs. Schultz, her eyes bulging, while Nano walked next to Charly with his head lowered. June followed them from a safe distance. Once they had reached the ring, Summer began running wildly in circles as Mrs. Schultz tried to mount her.

"Should I hold onto her?" asked June, who stood by her side.

"Yes, that would be a big help," said Mrs. Schultz gratefully. June held the reins with one hand, and the right stirrup with the other, so that the saddle wouldn't slip out of place. Once Mrs. Schultz was finally on Summer's back, she took the reins and rode off. Summer immediately began trotting and her owner had a hard time slowing her down to a walk. She almost bumped into little Nano who was calmly walking with loose reins.

"Now do you see who is injuring whom?" asked Charly. She gave her mother a dirty look.

"You need to do a better job of looking where you're riding," retorted her mother, who was annoyed as she tried to calm down her mare. "It's okay, sugar." After Summer rode a few rounds with more or less loose reins, Mrs. Schultz took up the reins and began to trot. June could hardly believe the enormous strides with which the chestnut mare floated over the ring. She really looked like she was wearing seven-league boots. There was no question about it; Summer truly was a fine horse, even though she was a bit too nervous. The more she trotted, the more she got into it and gave it her all, lengthening her strides. Mrs. Schultz's face was already red from the exertion of trying to keep her mare under control. It was the total opposite of Nano, who took small strides, trotting in a perfectly measured rhythm and snorting with satisfaction every few yards.

June noted with admiration that he and Charly had learned quite a bit in the past few months. She rode a lot of serpentines and walk-trot transitions that Nano mastered skillfully and then continued onwards, snorting in satisfaction.

The situation was quite different with Summer and Mrs. Schultz. Although Charly's mother was a good rider, the mare was so worked up that she hardly had a chance. Regardless of how much she tried to work with Summer, the mare kept pulling her head up and whinnying shrilly. Mrs. Schultz's calming words were of no use.

Charly kept shooting annoyed glances in their direction, with a dark expression on her face. June wondered what was eating her. Nano didn't let Summer's carrying-on disturb him in the least and happily continued his rounds.

Then Charly began riding the full ring, while her mother tried to get Summer under control in the circle. She wasn't having much success and just as Charly passed by with Nano, the mare bucked sideways and bumped into the Haflinger.

"Would you be a little more careful!" shouted Charly nervously, as she slowed Nano down to a walk.

"Charly, do not use that tone of voice with me," rasped Mrs. Schultz as she shortened the reins some more. "You can see perfectly well that Summer is nervous. Quit riding so close to her."

"Who is riding too close to whom?" hissed Charly. "Summer should just behave herself. Nano is able to keep himself under control."

"Charly, Summer is an extremely well-bred sport horse and Nano is a pony. You can't compare the two," Mrs. Schultz said in a patronizing tone of voice, while she chased another round in a canter.

"How many times do I have to tell you that Nano isn't a pony, he's a Haflinger!" Charly shouted, throwing the reins down on the chestnut's neck. "I'm tired of riding with you. Go ride by yourself."

Without even giving her mother or June another glance, she rode out of the ring. At that Summer lost more composure and began whinnying shrilly again.

June watched Mrs. Schultz for another minute and then turned to walk over to the courtyard, where Charly had already taken off Nano's saddle.

"Hey."

"Hey," grumbled Charly. "That stupid Summer. She always has to put on a show."

"She can't really help herself," June said, trying to placate her friend. "All this is totally new to her. No wonder she's so nervous."

"Summer is always nervous," Charly murmured. "It bugs me that my mother always acts like the world revolves around her horse. Nano may not be as fancy as Summer, but at least he's not going to break anyone's neck."

"Summer's not all that bad, either," laughed June. "You'll see, she'll calm down soon enough, after we take her up to the paddock this afternoon."

"You really think so?"

Charly looked at her doubtfully.

"Of course," said June confidently. "Just wait until she's gotten used to things here. Then she'll never want to leave."

Chapter 14

April sat on the bed and stared out of the window to the courtyard where Charly was in the process of taking off her Haflinger's saddle. She glanced at the clock. They couldn't have been in the ring for very long. And what had happened to the elegant chestnut mare that was with them? Good grief, April, she scolded herself in her thoughts, now quit thinking about horses all the time. You've seen what good it does you. Being led around like a baby on a little walk. Rightly so. At this point she didn't even have the confidence to trot anymore. She promised herself that as soon as the week was over, she would never have anything to do with horses ever again. Never again!

April swallowed. She wished she call home right away and ask to be picked up. But that wasn't possible. She didn't want anyone to see that she regretted insisting upon going on this vacation. Least of all her parents, who worried too much about her as it was. After this, she would close the book on the topic of riding once and for all. She lay on her back in bed and closed her eyes. She lay there for quite some time, and then the door opened.

"April?"

Ben stood in the doorway.

"May I come in?"

April wanted to be alone, but didn't dare to say so. She nodded wordlessly.

"I, er, just wanted to say again that you can talk to me any time if something is bothering you, okay?"

"Do you take care of all you guests this way? Or why am I getting all the special treatment?" April asked scornfully. Ben looked stricken and she immediately regretted what she had said.

"We just want for all our guests to feel comfortable here," said Ben quietly. "That goes for you as much as it goes for anyone else here. So if anything is bothering you, then please say so."

"It's nothing, okay?" said April and looked at the floor. Good grief, this was embarrassing! Why couldn't they just leave her be? How desperately she wished that the week were already over. "Anything else?"

"Yes, I came to pick you up for our outing," said Ben. Without saying another word, he pushed her wheelchair next to her bed and reached out his hand to her. "Come on. Ines and Elli are waiting."

April had intended to back out of going on the excursion, but Ben didn't give her the chance. Reluctantly she took his hand and sat down in the wheelchair. Flori and Navajo were already saddled and waiting in the courtyard. Navajo had on the surcingle with the two grips.

"There you are finally," said Ines. "Elli can hardly wait to get going. Okay, up you go." Ines heaved her onto Navajo's back and they set off. The small powerful chestnut ambled peacefully next to her. Behind her Ben led an excited Elli on Flori.

"Wow, my first trail ride," the little girl squealed happily. "I can't wait to tell my mother."

April couldn't help but smile. She remembered how she had felt when she had gone on her first trail ride. In fact, Elli reminded her a lot of how she felt when she was still a little girl. Back then when the world was still in order. The memories swirled through her head until they were interrupted by a shrill whinny. April looked around, startled.

"What was that?"

"Oh, I'm afraid that was Summer. Mrs. Schultz wanted to bring her to the paddock."

Sure enough, they could see the chestnut mare walking around a section of the grassy field that had been marked off, her head high in the air.

"Why is she all worked up?" asked April.

"It's her second day here," explained Ben. "She's outside today for the first time. Normally she's in a big stable in Washington, near the park. She's a real stable horse that doesn't go out very much. Mrs. Schultz says that she has been trained to Grand Prix level dressage."

April was impressed.

"Mrs. Schultz rides Grad Prix dressage?"

Ben shook his head, laughing.

"No, not Mrs. Schultz. Her horse trainer. Summer is one of those horses that are supremely well trained because most of the time her trainer rides her. Mrs. Schultz doesn't have that much time to ride herself, so she pays someone to do it for her."

"I can't believe Charly doesn't want to ride Summer," said April, remembering her earlier conversation with the girl.

Ben laughed out loud and could barely contain himself. April was confused. What was so funny about what she had just said?

"Sorry," Ben giggled. "I'm not laughing at you, it's just that Charly used to be scared to death of horses and never rode at all. She only started to learn recently, here at Sunshine Farm. Her parents had just split up and she was pretty down. But then she fell for Nano and since her father had a guilty conscience about the separation, he bought the horse for her."

April listened attentively.

"How nice for her that her father has enough money to just buy a horse for her," she said. "So she must be doing well now."

"More or less," replied Ben. "But I wouldn't say Charly is doing well. To be honest, she's still really down because of the separation, especially since her dad has already gotten himself a new girlfriend. And her mother doesn't have a lot of time for her because she has to travel so much for her job." He was quiet for a moment, then added, "You know, everyone's got problems."

April's face turned bright red from embarrassment. How did he mean that: everyone's got problems? Was he trying to tell her that she shouldn't make such a fuss? At least Charly was still able to walk, unlike herself, sitting helplessly on Navajo's back and letting Ines lead her around.

"Hey, look!" called Elli after all of them had been silent for a while. "The others are over there!"

The other riders appeared on the dirt path ahead of them as they returned from their trail ride. Marty was in front on a dark brown mare while June brought up the rear on her white horse, making sure no one got lost.

"How was it?" asked Ben as the group rode by them.

"Super," said Sven. "We even galloped, and Noel was just great."

"I told him he'd better behave this time," said Nellie who was riding directly behind him. "I wouldn't have been able to handle another stampede with Ninja. The trails here are just terrific, April. I've never seen anything this great. We rode all the way up to the big country road."

When she heard the words country road, April grasped onto the surcingle with all her strength. The images flickered past in her head. The falling tree. Bonaparte, who had been startled by it and bolted, so that she couldn't get

him under control again. The country road. She shook
herself to get rid of the horrible images. Now she wanted
nothing more than to turn around, but she didn't dare say
a word. As it was, she had the feeling that Ben thought she
was acting like a baby. If she were honest with herself,
then she couldn't really contradict him.

Chapter 15

"That was a terrific trail ride," said Charly after she had returned to the courtyard and tied up her horse next to June's.

"I told you so," June smiled. "It turned out to be a good day after all."

"Thank goodness. Earlier this afternoon I was so mad at my mom that I wanted nothing more than to go straight home again. At first I was so happy that she decided to come along, but right now I wish she were off on another business trip."

"Don't be so unfair," said June. She thought Mrs. Schultz was a little odd, but pretty nice overall. "If your mother hadn't come here to cook for us all week, we would have been in serious trouble. Not to mention that she's a sensational cook."

"I suppose that's true," Charly sighed and took off Nano's saddle. "Still, I have to say that she, well, I'm not sure how to say this, but she just doesn't fit in here. And Summer is even worse. Those two simply belong in a big city stable like the one in Washington. Out here my mother is a little embarrassing. What does your mother think of her, anyway? She probably thinks she's pretty weird, huh?"

"Maybe. But if there's one thing that my mother finds embarrassing in connection with your mother, then it would be herself."

"Really?" Charly stared at her. "But why?"

"Because you mother's always so perfect, the total opposite of my mom. She's always well dressed, her hair looks perfect, she has a terrific car, a super horse, a great career ... My mom rarely wears anything fancy, her hair is all over the place, she drives a pretty dirty car and although she has a great horse, it's not even in Summer's league. I think she feels pretty inferior next to your mother."

"Do you really think that she sees it that way?" asked Charly incredulously. "The whole time I was worried that I had to be ashamed of my mother in front of yours."

"You're not serious," said June while she curried Nelson's silky soft coat. "For you it's all normal stuff, but out here, your mother comes off as very formal." She thought for a moment and then continued. "Sometimes I wonder if I'd be ashamed next to you if we were in Washington."

"What?"

Charly could hardly believe her ears and was so surprised that the currycomb dropped out of her hand.

"You know, you live in that fancy house, take piano lessons, you don't smell like the stable – you know what I mean."

Charly shook her head.

"As for me not smelling like horses there, well, there's not much I can do about that because Nano lives out here with you. But if it were my choice, I would like nothing more than to smell like the stable every day. Aside from which I'm exactly the same person in Washington that I am out here, and you can bet on that – your best friend."

A big smile spread across June's face.

"And I'm your best friend."

"Hey, what put you two in such a good mood?"

Marty strolled across the courtyard and stopped when she had reached the girls.

"Oh, nothing," said June and giggled. "We've just concluded that we are what we are."

Marty scratched her head and gave them a quizzical look.

"I don't have to understand that, do I?"

"Maybe yes, maybe no," June answered mysteriously.

Marty thought about that for a minute, then shrugged her shoulders and turned away.

"I don't have any time for riddles right now. I have to go check on Summer. I hope that she's finally been able to calm down."

"What did you mean by maybe yes, maybe no?" Charly asked after Marty was out of earshot.

"I just meant that it isn't any different with my mom and your mother as it is with us. The two of them are what they are. And that's good, because think what it would be like if we were all the same."

At dinner, Mrs. Schultz had outdone herself again. She had cooked up Hungarian goulash with boiled potatoes and a green salad. In June's opinion, it was the perfect meal after such a long trail ride. Everyone dug in and chowed down happily. Even April, who was normally so reserved, seemed to have worked up an appetite from her ride. Ben was sitting next to her telling about all the mischief the Haflinger Gang had gotten into.

"Farmer Myers?" asked Mike. "Isn't that the man we saw today with the big tractor? But he seemed so nice."

"Yes, since then he has gotten a lot nicer," said Ben and began telling the story of how they had helped their neighbor catch the group of teens that had been tearing up his fields. "But that doesn't mean that he won't get really unpleasant if the Haflinger Gang gets loose in his corn again."

"You're always talking as if all the Haflingers ever do is get into trouble," complained Charly, "but Nano is the nicest horse in the entire world. And I think that Navajo has been really wonderful during this vacation, too, don't you agree, April?"

"What?"

April looked up in surprise. She obviously hadn't been paying attention to what the others were talking about.

"I said that Haflingers are really wonderful horses, don't you think so?"

"Um, yes, they're quite nice."

"Quite nice?" said Charly, taking offense. "I think they're fantastic. Simply the best horses there are."

"Could you maybe talk about something other than horses?" Ben interrupted. "What do you say we have a Trouble tournament after dinner?"

Everyone cheered his suggestion, except for April.

"If you don't mind, I'd rather go to bed," she said and looked uneasily at the group. "That ride made me really tired."

"All right," said Ben with disappointment. "I'll take you right over to the dairy kitchen."

"You can leave that to me," Marty interjected. "I have to go feed the horses anyway, so I can take April with me."

"Wait for me, I'm coming too," called Mrs. Schultz. "I'd like to bring Summer to her box now. She's been outside long enough."

June quickly got the Trouble game out of the living room while Ben drew lots for who'd be playing against whom. During summer vacation, they always played board games outside under the old chestnut tree in the middle of the courtyard, but in the springtime the evenings were simply too cool.

"Okay then," said Ben and explained the rules. "We always play two against two until at the end there are only two people left. Then they'll play against each other for the championship of the tournament.

We'll play by elimination – whoever loses is out of the tournament."

They played a really exciting tournament and at the end Sven and Nellie were the last players left. It was anybody's game until the very end, but then Nellie managed to win by a hair.

"Congratulations to our new world champion!" called Ben and head Nellie's arm in the air, as if they were standing in the boxing ring. "What do you think, guys? Is anyone up for another go?"

Everyone wanted to play again and so it was only June who noticed Marty coming upstairs again. Marty got the orange juice out of the fridge and poured herself a glass. June stood up from the table and went over to her.

"Everything okay?" she asked quietly. "You look like you've got something on your mind."

Marty shrugged her shoulders.

"I'm not really sure," she whispered. "Something is not right with Summer."

"What do you mean?" asked June. "Did she injure herself?"

"No." Marty took a big gulp from her glass and shook her head. "She's so quiet now, almost apathetic."

"What does Charly's mother say?"

"Vanessa thinks that she's just tired after all the excitement."

"There, you see. She must know her horse well enough to see when something is really wrong."

"I hope so, I really hope so," said Marty pensively.

Chapter 16

When June woke the next morning and looked out of the window, she saw a silver-gray jeep parked in the driveway. It was Dr. Schell's car. What could he be doing here this early in the morning? Then it hit her like a ton of bricks. Didn't Marty say yesterday that there was something strange about Summer? June slipped into an old sweatshirt and a faded pair of jeans and raced down the stairs. At the back door, she slipped on her stable shoes and walked over to the stable where Mrs. Schultz, Marty and Dr. Schell were standing in front of Summer's box.

"What's wrong?" she asked nervously.

Marty turned around. She had dark circles under her eyes and looked as if she were very worried.

"Summer has colic. Dr. Schell has already been here for an hour, but she isn't feeling any better."

June looked over at Mrs. Schultz, who was holding Summer by her halter and stroking the nostrils of her mare, who seemed totally apathetic. Her eyes were totally red, as if she had been crying. June felt incredibly sorry for her. She thought about how upset she would have been if Nelson were sick.

"But how would she have gotten that?" asked June. "She got the same fodder that she always gets in Washington."

"It's probably all the excitement," said Marty sadly. "It must have all been too much for the poor thing."

"And it's all my fault." Mrs. Schultz sounded like she would break out in tears any minute. "Why didn't I leave her in her box in Washington and come here without my horse? I imagined that it would be so wonderful to be able to go on trail rides here together with Charly."

Now Mrs. Schultz really did start to cry. Marty put her arm around her shoulder and hugged her tightly.

"Vanessa, don't go blaming yourself. We have no idea if it was the excitement or not. Maybe it was the change in weather. There are a thousand factors that can cause colic. Dr. Schell will do everything he can for Summer to make her feel better soon."

Mrs. Schultz laid her head on Marty's shoulder and sobbed freely. June noticed that her mother suddenly wasn't inhibited in Mrs. Schultz's presence. Typical Marty. When the going got tough, you could always count on her.

Dr. Schell turned to Marty.

113

"I think that we need to insert a nostril-gullet probe."

"A nostril-gullet probe?" asked June and followed Dr. Schell to his car. "What in the world is that?"

"The horse will have a tube inserted into its nose that will go down into its stomach and then we'll drip paraffin oil into it. That will work to dissolve the blockage and take care of her constipation."

"Through the nose into the stomach?" June shuddered at the thought. "That doesn't sound very pleasant at all."

"It isn't," said Dr. Schell dryly. "But it helps. Here, hold this."

He pressed a foot-long wooden rod into her hand. It had a loop on one end.

"A twitch? Is that really necessary?"

"If it weren't I wouldn't be doing it," retorted Dr. Schell, while he continued to root around in his trunk. "The mare shouldn't move while I'm leading in the probe, otherwise she'll get injured internally on top of everything else."

June sighed. She knew that contrary to what people used to think the twitch didn't cause any pain. Rather, it caused endorphins to be released so that for a while the horse didn't feel any pain at all. Still, it looked pretty darn awful when the loop was wrapped around the horse's upper lip.

"Now don't look at me that way," warned Dr. Schell. "It's the best thing for her."

June followed Dr. Schell back to the box where Marty and Mrs. Schultz were still standing with Summer

Dream. It was only now that June noticed how much the mare was sweating so that her coat looked more black than dark brown. Dr. Schell went into the box and asked Mrs. Schultz to hold on to her mare, while he carefully wrapped the loop around Summer's upper lip. Then he pressed the wooden rod into Marty's hand. Next he took a rubber tube that had a diameter of about half an inch and led it into Summer's nose. The mare rolled her eyes and grunted, but stood completely still. Dr. Schell pushed the tube further and further. June thought the whole thing looked pretty nasty, but Summer didn't even flinch. Once a large section of the tube was in Summer's body, Dr. Schell took a funnel, set it on top of the tube and slowly poured in a liquid from a white canister.

To June it seemed like he was pouring in an endless amount and wondered how much could fit into the mare's body. Then Dr. Schell finally set down the canister and carefully pulled out the tube. When that was done, he gently removed the twitch and stroked Summer's forehead.

"That's a good girl."

"What happens next with her?" Mrs. Schultz asked fearfully.

Dr. Schell looked at Summer thoughtfully.

"Now we just have to wait and see if the treatment helps her. Would it be possible to stand her on wood chips?"

Marty nodded.

"I have chips here."

"Good. And don't give her anything to eat. I have to

go to the clinic now, but I'll stop by to take another look at her around noontime. If she takes a turn for the worse you'll have to call me right away."

The veterinarian packed up his instruments, stowed them in his trunk and then drove off.

"Alright then," said Mrs. Schultz and rolled up the sleeves of her mint green sweater. "I'll go take the straw out of her box and spread wood chips."

June gave Marty a surprised look. Never in her life could she have imagined that Mrs. Schultz would hold a pitchfork in her hands. But Marty put a quick end to that.

"I understand that you'd like to take care of your horse," said Marty gently, "but couldn't June and Charly take care of things in the box while the two of us see to breakfast? You can't let down all those children. And if I were to make breakfast, we'd never have guests at Sunshine Farm again."

Despite all her worries, a faint smile appeared on Mrs. Schultz's tear-stained face.

"Okay," she said and allowed Marty to lead her back to the house. June quickly tied up Summer so that she wouldn't be able to eat any of the straw and then fetched Charly, who by that time was already awake and dressed.

"Oh no," she said after June had told her what had happened. "My poor mother. And I was so mean to her yesterday."

"I'm sure she's forgotten all that by now. Come help me muck out Summer's box so that we can put down wood chips. I feel so sorry for the poor thing."

Compared to the day before, Summer Dream was just a shadow of herself. Her head hung as she stood tied up in her box, while June and Charly cleared out all the straw and took it in a wheelbarrow to the muckheap. Then they went to the storage closet next to the saddle room where Marty had a few sacks of wood chips.

"Why are we doing all this anyway?" grumbled Charly as they heaved one of the sacks into the wheelbarrow.

"So that Summer doesn't eat anything until she's feeling better. Her digestive system has to calm down before she can slowly get something to eat again. First we'll give her mash; that's good for her digestion."

"And why did she get colic?" asked Charly.

"My mom thinks that it may have to do with all the excitement," answered June. "Or maybe the change in weather from relatively cool to warm. They say that some horses get colic from that. I don't know if that's true or not. The only thing I do know is that it's pretty hard to figure out what caused it. There are lots of ways to get colic. The most important thing now is to make sure that Summer recovers from it. Your poor mother is totally upset."

When they got to Summer's box, they ripped open the plastic sack and distributed the wood chips throughout the entire box.

"I don't know," said Charly when they had finished and untied Summer. "I think straw looks a lot more comfortable."

"I think so, too, but for horses that aren't supposed to eat much or anything at all, wood chips are ideal," June explained as she closed the box door behind her. "And speaking of eating, I could use something to eat myself. Mucking out really works up an appetite, don't you think?"

"That's for sure," called Charly. "Last one there is a rotten egg."

Chapter 17

Fortunately, Summer's condition improved over the course of the day so that by afternoon she was able to eat a little mash and hay. Mrs. Schultz visited her in her box regularly and checked to be sure she was okay. In the evening, she led her around the ring for a little exercise. The mare seemed to be herself again and whinnied excitedly at the other horses the entire time. Mrs. Schultz tried to calm her down, but eventually gave up in frustration and led the mare back to her box.

"I had hoped that it would do Summer some good to breathe in the fresh country air," she sighed to Marty over dinner that night. "But now I just don't know what to do with that horse. I hope she doesn't get herself so worked up again that she ends up with another colic."

"Now quit blaming yourself all the time," said Marty.

"As I said, no one can ever tell you exactly why Summer got colic. She could just as well have gotten it if she had stayed in Washington. Who can know for sure? The important thing is that she's doing better now."

"Maybe she'd do even better if she weren't so alone," piped in June, who had overheard their conversation.

Marty and Mrs. Schultz looked at her quizzically.

"What do you mean by that?" asked Marty.

"Well, I was thinking that maybe she's afraid to be all alone in a strange environment. If she had a friend, it might be easier for her."

"A friend?" asked Charly's mother. "I can't imagine who might fit the bill."

June thought about it for a moment, then her eyes began to sparkle.

"How about opening up her box a bit and moving Nano in to spend the night next to her? Maybe that will comfort her. I mean, only if it's okay with Charly if we take him away from the rest of the herd.

"If it'll help Summer, then of course it's okay with me," said Charly. "I just wonder if your idea will really work."

"Why don't we try it out right now?" said June, who was feeling adventurous. "I bet that Summer will be thrilled not to have to spend the entire night alone in the stable."

Marty and Mrs. Schultz looked at each other.

"Do you have any reservations, Vanessa?"

"We could give it a try. Maybe June's right and it'll do Summer good to have some company."

June, Charly and Ben stood up in unison and raced out to the courtyard.

"I'll get Nano," said Charly. She grabbed a lead off a hook and ran over to the paddock where Nano was standing with his friends.

June and Ben walked into the stable and over to where two heavy wooden poles lay on the ground. The lifted them up and into the holding brackets that had been attached to the walls for them. Because there was always the possibility that more than one horse could be sick at the same time, Marty had come up with this construction some time ago. Next they went into the barn and hauled out two bales of hay. While they were strewing it on the floor of the second box, Charly crossed the yard with Nano. Summer seemed to be her old self again and whinnied a loud greeting. Charly stopped in front of her box to give the horses an opportunity to sniff each other. Summer drew back her ears a bit and squealed, but she seemed elated to have company. Then Charly led Nano to his new quarters and pulled the halter off over his head. He made a complete turn around, sniffed at the straw and then turned to Summer, who inquisitively poked her head over the small separation between their boxes.

"See? I knew it!" June laughed. "Summer needed company. Take a look; I think they like each other."

Much to the delight of everyone watching, Nano and Summer thoroughly sniffed each other and clearly decided that they liked each other.

"Who would have guessed little Nano would wind up with such a big girlfriend," Charly giggled. "I hope this doesn't go to his head."

Outside they heard footsteps on the gravel. The door opened and Marty and Mrs. Schultz entered.

"Well?" asked Marty. "How's it going?"

"Marvelously!" June pointed to Nano and Summer, who had put their heads together.

Marty laughed.

"Those two horses are a real kick! I'll bet you two never thought that your horses would turn out to be such good friends, huh?"

Charly and her mother looked sheepishly at each other.

"I'm so sorry, sweetheart," Mrs. Schultz said finally and gave Charly a hug. "I think your Nano is terrific. And I'm not the only one – take a look at Summer. She's fallen for him, head over heels."

Summer rubbed her head against Nano's and, for the first time since her arrival at Sunshine Farm, she looked pleased and happy.

"I'm sorry too, Mom," said Charly and slowly lowered her arms. "I shouldn't have spoken so poorly about Summer, just because she's so different from my Nano."

"You know what? We all just are what we are," said Mrs. Schultz, who looked utterly confused when June and Charly began to laugh wholeheartedly and were unable to stop.

Chapter 18

"Today we're going out again, right?" asked Ben as he brought April over to Navajo and Ines after lunch. "The weather sure is perfect for a trail ride."

April made a face and squinted into the bright spring sunshine. With a grumble, she acknowledged that a slow walk with Ines was once again the order of the day.

Elli and Flori wouldn't be joining them because the little girl had a bad stomachache and had to stay in bed and rest. Ben would care for her while the others went for a trail ride.

Ines had gotten Navajo ready herself since April hadn't shown the least bit of interest in participating. Nevertheless, the gelding seemed to be happy to see her and gently nudged her arm with his soft mouth.

"I think Navajo is pretty fond of you," Ines smiled as she tightened the surcingle.

April stroked the little chestnut's head and looked into his lively sparkling eyes. It wasn't his fault that she had expected this vacation week to be quite different than it had turned out.

"He's a nice horse," she said.

Without further comment, Ines helped her onto the Haflinger's back and set off. After walking next to the Haflinger for some time in complete silence, she handed April the reins.

"Here, you're in charge today."

"Me?" April was aghast. "What if he doesn't do what I want him to do?"

"Don't worry," Ines pointed to the lead line that was still attached to Navajo's snaffle bit. "If he doesn't take your commands then I've still got him on the line. But I don't think Navajo will pull any tricks with you. He seems to understand that he has to take care of you."

April didn't feel as confident as Ines did, but she took the reins in her hands and quietly clicked with her tongue.

"Let's go, Navajo."

The small, muscular chestnut slowly began to move.

"Just as I said," Ines smiled. "He knows exactly what he has to do. He really is a smart fellow. And Marty and June didn't believe he could do it."

"What do you mean, they didn't believe he could do it?" April wanted to know.

"The first time I came here, they wanted to give me Marty's horse."

"That beautiful dark mare?" asked April. "Why didn't they? Oh wait, I think I know why." Suddenly her voice took on a bitter tone. "No one wants to let someone like me ride such a beautiful horse."

Ines looked up at her with an expression of shock. "What did you just say? That's utterly ridiculous."

"Oh yeah? Then why am I sitting on the back of a dull old Haflinger and not on that beautiful mare?"

"First of all," said Ines, with a threatening undertone in her voice, "Navajo isn't some dull Haflinger, and I don't ever want to hear anything like that from you again, is that clear? Besides, if you want to blame someone that you aren't sitting on that mare, then blame me."

"Blame you? But why?"

"Because I told them that Modena simply isn't suited to being a therapy horse, that's why," Ines answered, clearly annoyed. "She is much too big and sensitive. It's true that she's a beautiful horse and really quite nice, but I can guarantee you that neither of us would have had much fun with her. Navajo makes a much better therapy horse. He's not too big, he's even-tempered, and he's incredibly intelligent. In my opinion, he's the smartest horse in all of Sunshine Farm."

"You're just saying that to make me feel better," April said in a tremulous voice. "It's obvious that no one wants to put someone like me on horses as special as Marty's or June's.

"What exactly do you mean by 'someone like you'?" Ines asked.

April stared at her angrily. What a stupid question!

"Just what I said, someone like me!" she screamed. "A cripple, you know? A cripple!"

She pulled so hard on the reins that she startled Navajo and he took a step to the side. Ines was taken by surprise by the sudden movement and was jerked aside by the lead that she was still holding onto tightly. She stepped into a hole, stumbled and then fell down in front of Navajo's hooves. The Haflinger took two steps backwards and then stood still. He snorted, with his nostrils flaring.

"Ines? Are you okay?"

Horror-stricken, April looked down at the small woman who lay on the ground, whimpering. April wanted to scream. All this was her fault. What had she done?

Chapter 19

"Ines?" April called again.

Ines sat up slowly, clutching her left ankle.

"Aargh!" she cried. "I can't move my foot anymore, it hurts so much."

"Can you stand up?"

April looked around, panic-stricken. There wasn't a soul to be seen anywhere. Now what was she supposed to do?

Ines balanced herself with her hand on the ground and stood up. But as soon as she put her weight on her left foot, she screamed in pain and sat down again.

"It's no use," she whimpered. "It must be broken."

"Then we should call the farm right away so that someone can come get us," April suggested.

"Good idea," said Ines. "Do you have a cell phone with you?"

"What do you mean? Don't you have one?"

"No, I'm one of the few people in this world who doesn't carry a phone with her all day and all night. I can't stand those things."

"That's silly. I left mine on my bed because I figured I wouldn't need it out here."

Ines grimaced in pain and shuffled on her backside over to some shade trees at the edge of the path.

"At least the sun doesn't blind me here. Okay, let me get this straight. Neither of us brought along a cell phone, right?"

April nodded.

"Now what do we do?" she asked. "Do you think you could sit behind me on Navajo's back, so that the two of us can ride back to the farm together?"

April shook her head.

"No, my foot hurts too much. I don't know how I could pull myself up onto Navajo's back. I'm afraid we've only got one option."

"And that would be?"

"You ride back to Sunshine Farm by yourself to get help."

"You want me to do what?!" April shrieked. "You're not really serious, are you?"

Ines nodded.

"Of course I'm serious. What else are we supposed to do? Right now it's still pretty warm out here, but in March the nights can get pretty cold. Do you want the two of us to freeze to death out here?"

"But I'm sure that the others will come looking for us when they notice that we haven't returned," April argued.

"Of course they will, but what makes you so sure that they'll find us right away? Do you have any idea how many trails there are out here? We really don't have any other choice. You have to ride back to the farm alone to get help." Ines looked at the sky. "And you need to hurry because it gets dark pretty fast this time of year."

April bit her lower lip and thought it over. As frightening as she found the idea of riding back to the farm by herself, it really did seem to be their only option.

"How do I know how to get back to the farm? I don't know my way around here at all," she said finally, sounding pathetic.

"Once you get going I'm sure you'll remember the way," Ines said confidently. "Don't you understand? This is our only option."

April swallowed. The thought of riding with Navajo through this unfamiliar territory was pretty scary, but she couldn't think of anything else.

"Now get going," Ines pressed her. "I don't feel like waiting here forever. Get moving and Navajo will see to it that you find the way home."

Ines reached up and removed the line from Navajo's snaffle bit.

April clicked with her tongue and, using the reins, turned Navajo in the direction they had come from. The Haflinger slowly set off.

"Good luck!" she heard Ines call out to her.

At first it was easy because the path led in only one direction, but at the next crossing, April didn't know which path to take. On the way out here, she had been too deep in thought to pay attention to where she rode.

"Brrr, Navajo." She pulled gently on the reins and the gelding immediately stopped.

"What do you think? Do we turn right, left, or keep going straight?" April thought it over for a moment and then decided to continue in the same direction. She clicked with her tongue and rode on, hoping that she wouldn't regret her decision.

Chapter 20

The powerful Haflinger made his way along the trail with fervor and April slowly began to feel more confident on his back. After she had ridden a while, a long grassy path appeared in front of her. In the past, she would have galloped off immediately. Maybe she could try trotting a little? April thought about it. She was only able to control Navajo with her voice and the reins since she wasn't able to give him cues with her weight or her legs. She wondered if that would be enough, or if the gelding would use the opportunity to make a break for it.

"What do you think, little fellow?" she whispered and then ran her fingers through Navajo's think blonde mane that moved with every step he took. Navajo snorted happily.

"Alright then. Let's give it a try."

April shortened the reins and clicked her tongue.
"Tee-rott, Navajo."

Without any hesitation whatsoever, the Haflinger set off
in a pleasant trot. April held onto the surcingle with one
hand and just let him trot. It felt so wonderful to be sitting
on a horse again and feel the wind in her nose. Ever since
her accident, April hadn't felt as free as she did at that
moment. Navajo trotted calmly and evenly and seemed
to wait for her next command. The grassy path seemed
endless. Without giving it much thought, April tightened
her grip on the surcingle and called out, "Gallop, Navajo."
The small, powerful chestnut reacted immediately and
began a slow gallop across the field. With every stride his
long mane bounced up in the air, just like April's heart,
that jumped for joy with him. She wasn't sure if it was
the wind that made her eyes tear or if it was tears of joy
running down her face, but none of that mattered. She
was simply happy. Not even in her dreams could she have
imagined that she could be this happy again.

She was almost disappointed when they reached
the next crossing and Navajo slowed down of his own
accord, first to a trot, and then to a walk.

"Ines was right," said April as she wrapped her arms
around the gelding's muscular neck. "You really are a
smart horse. The smartest horse in the entire world."

Navajo snorted, as if in agreement. April thought
about which direction she should take now. Did Navajo
know the way? Then she remembered that Navajo liked
to break out of the farm to run free in the fields. He could

take her anywhere! After a brief moment of hesitation, she turned onto the path that led to the right. Shortly thereafter, they reached the edge of the woods. The dry pine needles on the wide path crunched underneath the Haflinger gelding's hooves. April breathed in the spicy forest air and looked up at the tops of the trees that were waving gently in the wind. The sunlight shone through the branches and made golden spots on the mossy forest ground. Navajo continued on conscientiously without even getting a little too fast. April had the feeling that she had known him forever. When they came out at the other end of the woods, the path led to a smaller trail that went straight through the cornfields.

"Let's go, Navajo, faster!" she called and held tightly onto the surcingle. The little chestnut extended his stride and practically flew with her over the grassy trail. He periodically snorted with satisfaction and seemed to be having as much fun as his rider. At the end of the trail, April easily slowed him down to a walk. Right or left?

Suddenly she felt a chill go up her spine. In her euphoria, she had forgotten that on the way out, they hadn't passed through any wooded areas. She couldn't remember having seen a cornfield either. That meant that they had gone the wrong way! She had no idea where they were. Now what should she do?

"Okay little fellow," she whispered and loosened the reins. "Now you have to decide which way we're going. Do me a favor and take us back to the farm, okay? We need to find Ines again before it gets dark."

Without any hesitation, Navajo went to the left and April simply allowed him to lead. She could only hope that the gelding knew the way back. This time she kept Navajo to a walk so that she wouldn't oversee any crossing. The way back seemed to take forever and she almost thought that Navajo had gone the wrong way, but then she saw Sunshine Farm in the distance. As they got closer, she saw that the others were already back from their excursion. She must have been out with Ines for a much longer time than it seemed. When she finally reached the farm, she brought Navajo to a stop. Ben noticed her first and ran up to her, full of concern.

"April, what are you doing here all alone? Is everything okay? Why were you out there alone? Did anything happen to you?"

April interrupted his flood of questions and explained to him what had happened.

"Can you describe where you left Ines?" Ben asked.

April thought about it for a moment and tried her best to remember everything.

"Unfortunately I got lost along the way," she said contritely, "so I don't know exactly how to get back there."

"Don't worry about it," Ben said soothingly. "Just try to describe to me what the spot looks like where Ines is waiting."

April thought back and tried to remember.

"There's a path through the fields," she said finally. "There are thousands of them here in the area. Lots of fields, and in the middle of them there's a path. The only thing I can really remember is the trees."

"What kind of trees?" asked Ben.

"Little trees. Or were they maybe bushes? At any rate, that's the only thing there is there."

"Do you think they might have been elderberry bushes? Ben asked.

April shrugged her shoulders. "Could be," she said. "Botany was never one of my strong points."

"That must be it," said Ben, "because there aren't really any other trees along the trail. We'll go take a look right away. Come on, I'll help you down."

"Why down?" April asked. "I'm coming along, of course!

"Do you really want to ride all the way back?" Ben asked with surprise.

"I already rode one way all alone," smiled April. "Well, not totally. Without Navajo's help, I would never have made it. He really is the best horse in the entire world."

"Okay, then you wait here and I'll go get Marty. We have to hurry now, before it gets dark."

Shortly thereafter, June on Nelson and Charly on Nano rode over to her. Ben had already told them all about what had happened and they were supposed to ride with April to get back to Ines.

"My mom will drive slowly behind us in her car. Then she can take Ines straight to the hospital. We'll ride next to you so that you don't have to ride back all alone," June explained.

137

"Okay."

April turned Navajo around again and clicked with her tongue. The gelding seemed to know exactly what they needed from him. Without any trouble, he trotted along the path through the fields. June and Charly looked at each other in surprise and followed behind. Before long, they had reached Ines who sat at the side of the path, grimacing. Marty jumped out of the car and took a quick look at her right foot.

"That definitely looks broken," she said. "I'll take Ines to the hospital for an X-ray; you girls ride back to the farm. See you later."

"See you later!" April called out and added, "Good luck, Ines. I'm really sorry."

"Sorry?" asked June, after Marty had loaded Ines into her car and driven off.

April told her what had led to the accident.

"Because I was being so stupid, Ines has to go to the hospital now," April groaned. "If only there were some way that I could make it up to her."

"Oh, I wouldn't worry about that," June grinned and winked to Charly. "Sometimes experiences like that lead to the best possible outcomes."

"What do you mean by that?"

June told her the story of how she had broken her shoulder because of something Charly did and then couldn't start in the tournament that she had been looking forward to.

"And look at what happened to us," Charly laughed. "Now we're best friends."

"By the way, have you noticed that Navajo was involved in both incidents when someone broke something?" asked June as she gave the Haflinger an accusing look.

"But it wasn't his fault this time," April defended the chestnut. "If I hadn't jerked the reins, he wouldn't have been startled and Ines wouldn't have ..."

"Wouldn't have, wouldn't have, wouldn't have," Charly laughed. "It doesn't really matter. Ines's foot will heal again, and anyway, there's a bright side to all this. If she hadn't broken her foot you wouldn't be sitting on Navajo like this, cool as a cucumber, and riding like you've never done anything else in your life."

"You did ride before, didn't you?"

June looked at April, unable to hide her curiosity.

"Yes, until ... until the accident." April cleared her throat. "I had a horse I took care of named Bonaparte. He was an extremely elegant Oldenburg gelding, who boarded in a riding stable near where we live. He was an incredibly beautiful golden chestnut, with a white blaze and four white feet. His owner didn't have much time for him so I took care of him most of the time. Bonaparte meant everything to me. I was with him nearly every day and even rode him in tournaments. We liked jumping most of all. It was the best time in my life."

She took a deep breath and added, "If you don't mind, I'd just like to enjoy riding Navajo right now.

I'll tell you the whole story when we're back at Sunshine Farm."

"That's a good idea," June said and pointed to the straight path through the fields ahead of them. "What do you say, want to do a little trotting?"

Chapter 21

Once they arrived back at Sunshine Farm, they were received by the other camp guests who wanted to know exactly what had happened. June and Charly took the saddles off their horses while Ben helped April to take care of Navajo and lead him to the paddock. If was a while before things had calmed down again and the three girls were able to sit down under the chestnut tree to relax. June and Charly took a seat at the table while April stayed in her wheelchair and gazed upwards into the sky.

"As I was saying, the time with Bonaparte was the best time of my life."

April paused for a moment and closed her eyes.

"And then?" Charly asked quietly.

"Then came the day that my friend suggested that we

ride around the outside of the paddock after our riding lesson was over. I didn't really feel like it, because it was pretty stormy outside, but I went along anyway."

April shuddered. "If only I hadn't gone."

She wiped a tear from the corner of her eye and continued. "Our ride around the paddock led past a small patch of woods. By the time we reached it, the wind had picked up. One of the trees must have been rotted and the wind blew it down. It made a horrible crashing sound as it fell to the ground. My friend's horse reared up and she fell off. Bonaparte bolted and I couldn't stop him. There was a country road that went near our riding ring and Bonaparte raced straight for it. I pulled on his reins and shouted, but it was like he had gone completely mad.

"Afterwards I asked myself why I hadn't just jumped off when I saw the road in front of me. Instead, I stayed on him and let things happen around me. The moment Bonaparte ran onto the road, I heard a horn honking loudly and then a horrible crash. After that, everything went black, and the next thing I remember is waking up in the hospital and seeing my parents sitting at the side of my bed. They didn't tell me until several days later that I'd never be able to walk again."

"That's terrible," June said sympathetically. "And what happened to Bonaparte?"

April took a deep breath.

"They told me later that when the car crashed into him, Bonaparte broke a leg and had to be put down right

143

there at the scene. And it was all my fault. At the time I thought that I would never ride again."

"But it wasn't your fault!" June cried. "It was just a terrible accident. You couldn't help that."

April shrugged her shoulders. "I've been trying to convince myself of that, but whenever I do, I have to ask myself what would have happened if I hadn't gone on that last ride."

"I understand what you mean," Charly said sympathetically and put her arm around her shoulder. "I'm always trying to imagine what my life would be like today if my parents hadn't gotten divorced. It may sound trite, but things just are the way they are and we have to find a way to accept that and live with it."

April smiled gratefully at Charly.

"You're probably right."

"And what made you decide to come to Sunshine Farm for vacation?"

"Good question." April thought for a moment. "Somewhere along the line I started getting interested in horses again and asked my parents to bring me some horse magazines. Then I saw your ad and, well, I guess it just sounded nice. You know – everyone gets her own horse to care for."

"But it wasn't exactly what you had in mind, was it?" June scrutinized her face. "I was afraid that you didn't like being here at all."

"At the beginning, that was true," April admitted haltingly, but added quickly, "But that had nothing to do with Sunshine Farm. I hadn't been prepared for how different everything would be."

She smiled at Charly apologetically.

"I used to think that Haflingers were just for beginners. I was so angry that I couldn't have a horse as elegant as Nelson or the mare that Charly's mother brought. On top of that, I felt so helpless on Navajo because I couldn't ride the way I used to. Besides, everyone else was allowed to ride freely, but I had to be led. Pretty stupid of me, huh?"

"Not at all," said June. "It would have been strange for anyone if they suddenly had to get used to doing everything so differently. Personally I think you're doing great. It was really courageous of you to ride back to the farm with Navajo the way you did."

"Gosh, Navajo did it all by himself," April said self-consciously. "He really is a terrific horse and I'm overjoyed that I can ride him. If it weren't for him I'd still be at home, sitting around in my room, being angry at the world."

"You see, and now you're even ready to go with all of us on a real trail ride," Charly said with satisfaction.

"Yes, that would be wonderful," April gushed. "I never would've been able to do all that without Sunshine Farm. I'm so grateful to all of you. And I'm sorry that I've been so hard on you."

"You weren't hard on us at all," said June. "Now the most important thing is that you enjoy riding again."

"Besides, this way we found out that Navajo is a perfect therapy horse," said Charly, adding reproachfully, "after being

145

underestimated for so long. The little fellow is just too smart to simply walk in a circle all day long. He needs a challenge – a real responsibility – and once he has a mission, you can rely on him one hundred percent. I've always said –"

She was interrupted by Ben, who suddenly came running across the gravel to them.

"June! You have to saddle up Nelson immediately and come with me. Farmer Myers just called. The Haflingers got out again and are standing around in his cornfield next to the paddock. He sounded pretty angry."

June snorted loudly.

"You're totally right, Charly, you really can count on Navajo one hundred percent. As soon as he gets back together with his gang, he goes back to his old mischievous ways." She laughed as she followed Ben into the saddle room.

"What are you planning to do after vacation ends?" Charly asked April after the other two had disappeared.

She shrugged her shoulders. "No idea. Go to school. Do homework."

"And what about riding?"

April sighed.

"I'll have to wait until the next vacation, although that's better than nothing. There aren't any stables near us where I can ride. More importantly, there aren't any with a horse as wonderful as Navajo. But at least now I know that he's around and that I might be able to see him again soon."

Chapter 22

"What a shame that the week is already over," June said to Charly. "But when Cheryl Morris gets back, we can't tell her how wonderfully you mother cooked for us. I'm sure she'd be very offended."

The two girls stood at the paddock fence and observed Navajo, Nino, Ninja and Noel who stood under the fruit trees and grazed with satisfaction.

"What do you think Nano will do when he gets separated from Summer later?" April asked. Charly shrugged her shoulders.

"No idea. He'll probably miss her, though. The two of them have really gotten accustomed to each other these past few days.

It was true. In that short time, little Nano and monumental Summer had become inseparable. Summer seemed to have undergone a real transformation ever since she'd been put in the paddock with Nano. Charly and her mother had even been able to take them on relaxing trail rides over the past few days without any problems at all.

"I still feel sorry for Summer," Charly added. "At least Nano gets to hang out with his buddies on the paddock and can stay here at Sunshine Farm, but Summer has to spend most of her time just standing in her box. She doesn't go out for many rides, either."

Two cars drove into the courtyard and parked in front of the residence. Nellie's and Sabrina's parents had arrived. The two girls ran over to say goodbye.

"See you soon!" Nellie called out again as she got into the car. "I know we'll be back again sometime!"

June and Charly waved to them until the two cars drove around the curve and out of sight. More cars pulled into the courtyard. June sighed. As she did every time, she felt a pang of regret as she watched their guests drive off. In just a week, she had gotten used to having them around and she knew that she would miss them when they were gone.

June saw April's mother and father standing with Marty. They looked relaxed and relieved. They seemed happy to hear that April wound up having such a good time after all. April waved to them from a distance with broad smile lighting up her entire face.

"Want to bet that we'll see her again next vacation?" asked June.

Charly laughed.

After all of the other campers had been picked up, Mrs. Schultz parked her dark blue BMW in front of the house and, with Marty's help, carried her bags downstairs. Marty had invited her to stay over the weekend, but she had an important appointment in the city that she couldn't cancel. June was relieved that Charly would be staying the weekend because without her it would've suddenly felt incredibly lonely at Sunshine Farm.

"When is the horse trailer coming?" Charly asked.

Mrs. Schultz gave her daughter a surprised look. "What trailer?"

"The one picking up Summer, of course."

"Oh, didn't I tell you?"

"Tell me what?" asked Charly, who had no idea what was going on. "Come on, Mom, go easy with all the suspense," she begged her.

Mrs. Schultz and Marty looked at each other and laughed.

"Well, since I enjoyed our rides together so much, I thought it would be a shame if we weren't able to do that again."

"And?" Charly pressed.

"That's why I talked things over with Marty and decided that Summer will spend the summer here at Sunshine Farm."

"Summer is staying at Sunshine Farm?" Charly couldn't believe it. "And when are you going to ride her?"

"That all depends on my work schedule, but I thought

it made more sense for our two horses to board at a stable together. Summer will be happier spending time on the paddock here with Nano than staying in her box in Washington waiting for the trainer to take her out. Besides, since it stays light out until late in the evening during the summer, we could easily drive out here together for an early evening ride. What do you think?"

Charly hugged her mother tightly.

"What do I think? That's the best thing I've ever heard!"

"I was asked to report to Mr. Kemp."

"The principal has someone in his office right now, you'll have to wait a moment. What is your name, please?"

"Jasmina Blum."

The secretary looked at her sternly.

"Oh, so that's who you are. Well, sit down over there."

She pointed to the chair directly next to the office door.

Jasmina sat down and waited. She could hear voices coming from the principal's office. This could take a while.

Jasmina sighed deeply. Why did this have to happen now, of all times? She had finally convinced her parents to let her go to horseback riding camp – and then this. No matter what she said no one would believe that she didn't do it, or that she didn't know who put her classmate's iPod into her school locker. She unzipped her backpack, took out a magazine and read the advertisement that she had read so often over the past few days:

Horseback riding camp in idyllic Upper Marlboro for boys and girls, 8-16 years of age. Affectionate care, exceptionally beautiful grounds for trail rides and riding instructions with well-trained ponies and horses guaranteed. Lodgings in our picturesque farmhouse. All guests will have their own horse or pony to care for. Contact: Marty Sunshyne, sunshine@horsemail.com, Tel. ...